W9-CPN-932

FROM THE
NANCY DREW FILES

THE CASE: Nancy's determined to find out why Annie Goldwyn, a woman who wanted to save the environment, ended up losing her life.

CONTACT: Jonathan Winston, *director of the aquarium, believed in Annie's cause and now wants her killer brought to justice.*

SUSPECTS: Stuart Feinstein—*Annie's boyfriend worked for one of the companies she was investigating . . . and he has suddenly disappeared.*

Chris Marconi—*the aquarium shark expert is a bit of a lady's man who never forgave Annie for refusing to go out with him.*

Megan O'Connor—*She always thought she would get the curator job . . . but was passed over in favor of Annie Goldwyn.*

COMPLICATIONS: Even after Annie is murdered, the aquarium continues to receive death threats, and the next in line to take a dive is Nancy Drew!

Books in The Nancy Drew Files® Series

THE NANCY DREW FILES™

Case 68
CROSSCURRENTS

CAROLYN KEENE

AN ARCHWAY PAPERBACK
Published by POCKET BOOKS
New York   London   Toronto   Sydney   Tokyo   Singapore

AN ARCHWAY PAPERBACK *Original*

An Archway Paperback published by
POCKET BOOKS, a division of Simon & Schuster Inc.
1230 Avenue of the Americas, New York, NY 10020

ISBN: 0-671-73072-X

First Archway Paperback printing February 1992

10 9 8 7 6 5 4 3 2 1

Cover art by Tom Galasinski

Printed in the U.S.A.

IL 6+

Chapter

One

LOOKS LIKE you've found an admirer, George,"
Nancy Drew teased. She pulled up her coat collar
to ward off the brisk March wind that swept in
from the nearby inner harbor and blew her
reddish blond hair into her eyes.

"I'm sure he's a better swimmer than most of
the guys I date," George Fayne answered, laughing. She leaned against the low stone wall of the
seal pool at the National Aquarium in Baltimore,
smiling at the huge spotted seal that had crawled
onto a rock a few feet away. "Look at those sweet
black eyes," she added.

As if embarrassed by the attention, the seal
grunted, twisted off the rock, and dove into the
pool of clear water. His hind flippers hit the
surface with a clap, sending a cold splash in
George's direction.

"Whoa!" George gasped, jumping back and brushing a few drops from her short, curly dark hair. "Was it something I said?"

"Maybe that's his way of being friendly," Nancy suggested.

Both girls looked up as a young woman climbed over the low wall that surrounded the seal pool. She was carrying buckets brimming with silvery fish and was wearing a jacket with the words *National Aquarium in Baltimore* printed on it.

"Oh, it's feeding time," Nancy said. She glanced at her watch. "Dr. Winston isn't expecting us until ten-thirty, so we have another fifteen minutes. We might as well stay here and watch breakfast being served."

"Raw fish." George wrinkled her nose. "Not *my* first choice for breakfast. I'm glad we had those muffins at the coffee shop in the hotel."

Nancy and George had taken a flight to Baltimore from Chicago the night before. On Saturday Nancy had received an urgent phone call from the aquarium's director, Dr. Jonathan Winston. Dr. Winston, an old friend of Nancy's father, Carson Drew, had mentioned a "problem" at the aquarium, but he had been hesitant to discuss it over the phone.

Nancy had readily agreed to meet with him on Monday morning. She had always wanted to see the famous aquarium, and this case would give her the perfect opportunity. Since George had been able to come along, Nancy hoped they would find time for fun as well as sleuthing.

As George mugged for the seals, Nancy leaned back and studied the aquarium building. Topped by a shimmering glass pyramid, it was a conglomeration of concrete squares, rectangles, and a single towerlike cylinder. A blue neon wave curled around the cylinder, and geometric shapes had been painted in bright colors on the lowest portion of the building.

"Welcome to the National Aquarium in Baltimore," the tall, slender young woman said to the small crowd that had formed to watch the feeding. She stood on a concrete patio between the seal pool and the angular aquarium building. Her voice was amplified with the help of a small microphone clipped to her jacket collar.

She tucked her wispy copper-colored hair behind her ears, then knelt down and threw a few fish toward the eager seals. "I'm Megan O'Connor, a marine mammalogist. As you can see, it's feeding time for our seals."

No sooner had Megan tossed out a few fish than the whole pack began to stir. They flopped off the rocks and swam over to her.

Megan stood on a stone platform and wiggled a dead fish at her feet. One seal wobbled out of the water and inched toward her. "This is Lady," Megan explained. "She's a gray seal, and she's going to vocalize for you."

On cue, the seal began to grunt and growl. The audience laughed at the piglike noises.

"Lady is definitely not a soprano," Nancy joked.

"Lady is demonstrating the sound that all seals

3

make," Megan told the crowd. "We know that seals call to one another. They are social animals, and they love company."

As Nancy watched, Lady took a fish as her reward, then dove back into the water. Despite the seal's awkwardness on land, underwater she was as graceful as a dancer.

Nancy was impressed at the way the seals responded to Megan. Continually using the fish as incentive, the young woman prompted the animals to do their tricks for the crowd. Each seal responded to his or her name. One zipped through the water at great speed. Another opened his mouth and displayed his sharp teeth. And Ike, the seal that had been flirting with George, used his hind flippers to splash the crowd.

"I guess Ike's a real party animal," George said as the seal sent another splash in her direction. George, who was lithe and athletic, had no trouble ducking the icy spray.

"Oh, look," said Nancy. She pointed to a baby seal that had leapt out of the water. It edged toward Megan's feet, then nuzzled her leg, just like an affectionate puppy. "Oohs" and "Aahs" rose from the crowd.

"Hi, Asia," Megan said, kneeling down to rub the seal between the eyes. "Asia is a two-month-old seal pup, our newest addition to the seal pool. Last week she weighed in at about eighty pounds."

"She's adorable!" commented George.

Nancy nodded, then glanced at her watch.

"Time to head inside," she told George, and turned away from the seal pool.

George followed Nancy to a walkway at the right of the pool. It led to the aquarium's private entrance, which Dr. Winston had described on the phone. The girls found the warm corridor to be a welcome relief from the cold, wet wind.

A long desk stood beside a staircase to the aquarium. Nancy approached the desk and spoke to the uniformed guard. "I'm Nancy Drew, and this is my friend George Fayne. We have an appointment with Dr. Jonathan Winston."

"If you'll just sign our guest book, I'll call upstairs," the guard said, sliding the book toward the girls.

Nancy and George signed their names, then looked around as they waited for the guard to finish his call. Nancy watched the monitors lined up on the wall in the guard's station. One screen showed the seal pool, where the mammalogist was still talking to the crowd. Although she wasn't familiar with the sights on the other monitors, Nancy thought she caught a glimpse of a group of triangular rays and a whale with a rounded nose.

The guard hung up the phone, handed badges to both girls, and motioned toward the staircase. "Dr. Winston's office is just upstairs and down the hall to your left."

Upstairs, Nancy and George made their way past office cubicles abuzz with the sounds of employees chatting, phones ringing, and computer printers clattering. "Where are the fish?" George asked.

"Don't worry, we'll see the rest of the aquarium," Nancy promised. "This is the stuff that goes on behind the scenes—the work you don't see."

Nancy was halfway down the hall when she noticed a stocky man with salt-and-pepper hair standing in the doorway of an office at the end of the corridor. He was nervously drumming his fingers on the doorjamb but stopped when he saw the girls.

"Nancy Drew?" A smile lit his face. "You must be. You have your father's eyes," he said, stepping forward to shake Nancy's hand. "I'm Jonathan Winston. I've heard a lot about you over the years. Carson thinks you could solve the mysteries of the world, given half a chance."

Nancy tried to ignore the heated blush that crept up her cheeks. "That's Dad for you," she mumbled, then quickly added, "This is my friend George Fayne."

"Pleased to meet you," Dr. Winston said to George, then gestured toward his office. "Please, come in . . . take off your coats and sit down. I just buzzed one of my curators, Annie Goldwyn, whom I'd like you to meet."

Warmed by the winter sunshine that streamed into Dr. Winston's office, Nancy and George took off their jackets and hung them on a rack in one corner. Nancy went over to the windows, which offered a view of Baltimore's busy harbor, and looked out for a moment. Then she turned back to the office. She noted that the furnishings were modest. A set of beige director's chairs faced a modern pine desk that was covered with files, memos, and photographs.

"I appreciate your making the trip here, especially on such short notice," Dr. Winston said. He closed the door and went over to sit behind his desk.

Nancy sat down in one of the director's chairs, and George took the chair beside her.

"You didn't say much over the phone," Nancy admitted, "but I sensed that this was important. And you mentioned a deadline . . ."

"Friday," he said, nodding gravely. "It's our ten-year anniversary, and we're planning a big bash here. It's our chance to thank the contributors whose financial donations have helped us over the years. And of course the press will attend, so it will be a publicity event, too."

Nancy counted off the days in her head. She had less than a week to unravel the case.

Dr. Winston's eyes darkened as he added, "If people get wind of the trouble we've been having, the future of this aquarium will be in jeopardy. So far, we've managed to keep things quiet, with the help of our discreet security force and some trusted employees. But I'm afraid word of our problems is going to leak out and attract some bad publicity."

Just then Nancy heard a knock on the door. As she glanced over, the door popped open and a young woman with tousled brown curls poked her head in. "It's just me," she said cheerfully.

7

"This is Annie Goldwyn," Dr. Winston said, and introduced her to Nancy and George.

The petite woman, who looked to be in her midtwenties, shook hands with both girls, then said to Nancy, "The boss told me all about you. I'm so glad you're here."

Annie had warm brown eyes and a pixie smile. She was a bundle of energy, and Nancy liked her instantly.

"We appreciate the welcome," Nancy said.

"And we're excited about seeing the aquarium," George added.

"Great! I think our little home has a few surprises to offer," Annie responded. "Even for two teen detectives."

"The detecting part is Nancy's department," George put in. "I just came along to keep her company."

"So," Annie said as she pushed aside a stack of papers and perched on the edge of Dr. Winston's desk, "have you folks gotten down to business?"

"Not yet," Dr. Winston said, shifting uncomfortably. He closed his eyes and rubbed his temples. Nancy could see that whatever the trouble was, it was taking a toll on him. "We've been receiving some threats—" he began.

"Menacing notes," Annie put in. "We think it's because of the Chesapeake Bay Task Force, a volunteer group I organized about a year ago to help clean up the bay and protect wildlife in our area. It's sort of a watchdog against pollution."

Dr. Winston stared out the window at a tugboat that was coursing through the gray-blue waters of the harbor. "Someone out there wants the task force stopped—immediately," he said gravely.

Nancy frowned. The scope of this case was bigger than she had expected. It wasn't just a matter of a problem at the aquarium. This was something that might affect the entire Chesapeake Bay area. "Did you save the notes?" she asked.

"Certainly." Dr. Winston reached into his desk drawer, pulled out a manila folder, and handed it to Nancy.

She rested the folder on her lap and opened it to study the first note. It was a plain white sheet of paper with a handwritten message in block print: " 'Kill the task force, or I'll kill the animals,' " she read aloud.

"That was the first one we received," Annie explained. "All of the notes promise trouble here at the aquarium if the task force isn't disbanded."

"Has this anonymous person followed through on any of the threats?" Nancy asked.

Annie nodded. "That's what really scares me. Last week, we found one of our birds—a scarlet ibis—with a skewer through it."

Nancy's stomach turned at the thought. This was the act of a truly sick mind. "Where was the bird found?" she asked.

"It was left on a rock in our South American rain forest exhibit, which you'll see later," Dr. Winston answered.

"What kind of person would kill an innocent bird?" George asked, looking disgusted.

Nancy was wondering the same thing. "Are you sure the dead bird was related to the threats?"

"There was a note attached to the skewer," Dr. Winston explained.

"I'll show you," Annie said as she took the folder from Nancy's lap and sifted through the papers until she pulled out a note that read: Victim of the task force. It was written with the same block lettering on plain white paper.

"That's an odd way to get the point across," Nancy said.

"Since then the notes have been vicious," Annie explained. "I've been finding them everywhere—on my desk, on my car, in my mailbox at home. . . ."

After a pause, she added, "I'm not about to disband the task force, but I'm beginning to get the creeps, and my boyfriend is getting antsy." She glanced over at Dr. Winston and added, "Stuart had a fit when he found one of the notes on the windshield of my car."

Dr. Winston frowned. "I had hoped to keep this problem from outsiders—in the family, so to speak. Do you think Stuart will tell anyone?" he asked.

"Don't worry about Stuart," Annie replied. "He can keep a secret. But I want to get to the bottom of this. And I don't want any more of our creatures to die."

Just then there was a sharp knock on the door, and in came a thin black woman. Nancy remembered seeing her in the cubicle next to Dr. Winston's office.

"This just came for Annie—by rush messenger," she said, smiling as she handed Annie an envelope.

"Thanks, Delores," Annie said. The woman nodded, then ducked back out of the office.

"As I was saying," Annie continued, tearing open the envelope, "we have to protect the . . ." Her voice trailed off, and her brown eyes widened with alarm.

"What is it?" Winston asked.

Annie didn't answer. She just stared at the note, which she clutched in one tight fist.

Moving to Annie's side, Nancy read the note aloud: " 'Kill the task force, or we'll kill Annie Goldwyn.' "

Chapter

Two

"THAT'S AWFUL!" George exclaimed.

"Are you okay?" Nancy squeezed Annie's shoulder sympathetically. She could understand why the young woman was frightened.

Annie shook her head in disbelief. "What a creep!"

"This is out of hand," Dr. Winston said firmly. Turning to Nancy, he added, "We must protect Annie at all costs. I wanted her to take some time off, but so far she's insisted upon facing the situation head on. But after this, I—"

"I can't run away and hide," Annie protested. "This is one battle I've got to stay and fight."

Nancy admired the young woman's courage. "I understand," she told Annie. "But this is a *personal* threat."

"I'll report it to the police just as I did the

12

other notes," Annie said, folding her arms, "but I'm not backing off."

"What about suspects?" Nancy asked, looking Annie in the eye. "Is there anyone you know of who has a grudge against you?"

Annie paused for a moment, biting her lip as she considered the question. "I've been trying to narrow it down. There's only one person I can think of who might get a kick out of scaring me. And that's Chris Marconi."

"Chris?" Dr. Winston's mouth opened in disbelief. "Chris Marconi is a curator here," he explained to Nancy and George. "But I find it hard to believe he's the one causing this trouble."

Annie shrugged. "I can't really accuse him, but I have to admit that we haven't seen eye to eye on things for quite a while. We don't agree on methods of animal care. He doesn't approve of the way the task force is being run. And he hates my boyfriend. It may sound petty, but I think that Chris could be the one behind the notes."

Dr. Winston was shaking his head. "I can't imagine a member of our own staff killing a bird in the rain forest."

"I hate to point the finger," Annie said, "but that's my honest opinion."

"And it's worth checking out," Nancy said, reassuringly. "In the meantime, can you use your security force to protect Annie?" she asked Dr. Winston. "At least she would be safe at work."

"I'll instruct them to keep a special watch over Annie. But the overall question of security—especially for the animals—is tricky."

Dr. Winston gestured toward the building behind him. "Our aquarium is vulnerable, to say the least," he admitted. "We have more than a million people touring the building each year, and we pride ourselves on allowing public access to the animals. We guard the animals carefully, of course, but a person probably could harm one of them if he or she were sneaky and careful enough."

"Did visitors have access to the bird that was killed?" Nancy asked.

"Yes, of course. Our birds are free to fly anywhere they like under the glass roof of the rain forest. As a general rule, we try to avoid caging our animals. And our visitors roam through the same area, which means that anyone could have captured the scarlet ibis."

"Let's face it," Annie said, pushing back her dark curls, "we're sitting ducks." A small smile lit her face. Judging from her pun, Nancy could see that Annie was recovering from the shock of receiving a death threat.

Nancy sat back in her chair and considered the situation. If she wanted to find out why someone was trying to stop the Chesapeake Bay Task Force, she needed to find out more about the organization. "Tell me about the task force," she said to Annie. "How many people are members?"

"Well, technically more than a hundred people are involved," Annie explained. "Whenever someone gives us a donation, we add his or her name to the roster. But there are only about a dozen active members, and most of them work here."

"I'd like to see a list of the members," Nancy suggested. "And maybe you can point out the key players for me."

"Sure, that's easy enough. I'll get you a copy of the roster right away."

"What about a headquarters?" George asked. "Does the task force have an office?"

"No," Annie responded. "We don't have the budget for that sort of thing. We usually meet in people's homes or in rented halls. Dr. Winston has let us meet here at the aquarium a few times, too."

"The aquarium and the task force are not officially linked," Dr. Winston explained. "But I guess you could say that we're simpatico."

"And what about the obvious enemies of the task force?" Nancy suggested. "Is there anyone who might have a grudge against the force? Maybe a group or an individual who's been fined or jailed because of crimes against the environment?"

"We *are* working on a project that has upset some people," Annie replied. "Although we don't yet have the proof we need, we're on the trail of two companies who've been accused of illegal dumping."

"What sort of companies?" Nancy pressed.

"The Mills Company, for starters. They manufacture tires," said Annie. "We've also been tipped off about a paper company named Paperworks, Incorporated. Since most illegal dumping occurs after dark, we've organized small groups to patrol the Chesapeake at night."

Nancy was impressed. "That's a lot of work."

"Yes, it is," Annie agreed. "It's not hard for me, though. I have a cabin cruiser, and I live right on the water. But so far, our patrols haven't come across any evidence."

"Does the task force have other enemies?" Nancy asked.

"We've been fighting over a few land sites that developers are trying to build on," Annie offered. "There's one developer, a woman named Lydia Cleveland, who's been giving us a problem. She's already had an architect draw up plans for a housing development on a large plot of water-front land called Terns Landing."

"What's wrong with people living right on the bay?" asked George.

"We have nothing against people," Annie explained. "But right now that land is home to countless wildlife—birds, fish, and frogs—you name it, it's living there. A housing development will put an end to those creatures."

"So the task force has had a few run-ins with Lydia Cleveland?" said Nancy.

"More than a few," Annie confirmed. "We're trying to have those areas declared wildlife sanctuaries."

Nancy nodded. She would check out the two companies and the developer. In the meantime, she was eager to learn the routine at the aquarium. She was surprised that the local reporters hadn't made a full-blown scandal out of the aquarium's problems, but it seemed that Dr. Winston had managed to keep things quiet. "What have the local police had to say about the threats? Do they have anyone working on the case?" Nancy asked Dr. Winston.

"There's a Detective DePaulo working on the case. Unfortunately, a few notes and a dead bird don't make it to the top of the police priority list."

"That's why the boss decided to call you," Annie added, looking Nancy in the eye. "So what do you think? Can you find this goon for us?"

"We need to know who's behind these threats," Dr. Winston added, "and I'd like to have the matter in hand before the press people flock in on Friday night. Can you help us, Nancy?"

"I'll give it my best shot," Nancy promised.

"Nan's a great detective," George volunteered. "She's solved some tough cases."

"That's exactly what Carson said." Jonathan Winston sat back in his chair and held up his arms in a gesture of helplessness. "We're in your hands, Nancy. I'll have my son Jackson show you around so that you can get a sense of how the aquarium is laid out."

"That's a great idea." Nancy stood up. "Judging from the shape of this building outside, I'll need a map to find my way around inside."

Dr. Winston picked up the phone and made a quick call to summon his son. Then he reached into his desk and pulled out two glossy booklets, which he held out to Nancy. "You'll find a map of the aquarium in these brochures."

Nancy took the brochures from Dr. Winston. "I'd also like your permission to roam freely through the building."

"Of course," Dr. Winston agreed. "We'll get you a key and some special visitors' passes."

A quick knock sounded on the door, and a moment later an athletic-looking young man strode into the office. Immediately, he took off his Baltimore Orioles baseball cap, revealing a head of short-cropped brown hair.

"Jackson is a junior in college," Dr. Winston explained, introducing the girls to his son. "He's spending this semester doing an internship here at the aquarium."

"I'll be glad to show you around," Jackson told Nancy and George.

Winston stood up, clapped his son on the back, then escorted the girls to the door. "You'll have access to any part of the building, and the staff will be at your disposal. I think you'll find that they're a cooperative group."

"And a young one," added Annie. "Most of our curators and assistants are in their twenties and thirties—some are just out of college."

George's brown eyes sparkled, and Nancy knew what her friend was thinking: With so many young people around, this case could turn out to be a lot of fun.

As the group filed out of the director's office, George and Jackson began to discuss the local sports teams. It looked as if George was already hitting it off with one member of the aquarium staff, Nancy thought, smiling.

When Dr. Winston followed the group into the hall, his secretary, Delores, rose from her desk in the adjoining office to intercept him. "Holly Payne is here to see you," she murmured discreetly. "*With* a camera crew."

"Oh, dear," Dr. Winston said, and ran a hand across his forehead. "In all the commotion, I nearly forgot."

"I asked them to wait in the conference room down the hall," Delores added.

After thanking his secretary, Dr. Winston told Nancy and George, "Holly Payne is a TV reporter for a Baltimore station. She's doing a piece on our anniversary, and I promised her an interview."

"In that case, we won't keep you any longer," Nancy said.

"Besides," added George, "I'm dying to get a look at this place."

As if preparing for battle, Dr. Winston raised his chin, took a deep breath, and stared at the conference room door at the far end of the hall. "I guess it's off to the lion's den for me. Care to join me, Annie?"

The young woman gave him a big smile. "When you put it that way, how could I say no?"

"Let's touch base before the end of the day," Dr. Winston said to Nancy. Then he lowered his voice and added, "Remember, the staff knows you're here, so you can speak freely with them. I trust my people. But let's try to keep this out of the public eye. The last thing we need is a scandal."

Nancy nodded.

"A scandal?" The words seemed to rise from the woodwork. "Shame on me for eavesdropping," said an unfamiliar voice.

A look of shock flashed across Dr. Winston's face, and Annie gasped. Nancy spun around to locate the person, who had been concealed in a nearby office cubicle.

A tall, willowy blond woman stepped out from behind the divider. "I just sneaked back here for a cup of coffee when you all burst out of the office," she said, holding up a cup.

"Holly . . ." Dr. Winston tried to cover his shock with a friendly smile. "We were just on our way to see you and the crew."

So this was Holly Payne, Nancy thought, taking in the woman's sleek platinum blond hair and red silk suit. Holly Payne looked every inch the sophisticated, inquisitive TV journalist, and at the moment, she was probing too close for comfort.

"The crew is getting some shots for the anniversary piece," Holly said, waving them off dismissively. "But this is a much juicier angle. What were you just saying about a scandal—or was that a vandal? It sounds like big news to me."

Chapter
Three

THE AIR SEEMED to sizzle for a moment as a tense silence surrounded the group.

Nancy forced herself to smile. She doubted that the reporter had been able to make out more than a hint of what Dr. Winston had been saying.

"I'm afraid he *was* talking about a scandal," Nancy said, easing into her story. "It's all very embarrassing—and very personal. We were speaking about my father, who's been a friend of Dr. Winston for nearly twenty years. And the scandal involves Dad and—" She hesitated and looked down at the floor, hoping that the reporter would buy her story.

Sorry, Dad, Nancy said to herself. Although Carson Drew was a great father, even he would not appreciate Nancy's little white lie.

21

"I think it's difficult for Nancy to discuss," Dr. Winston said, playing along with Nancy's ruse. He patted her arm sympathetically.

When Nancy glanced up, she caught an amused look from George. Nancy gave her a stern look, and George's grin quickly faded to a frown.

"Is that all it is—just a family scandal?" Holly Payne asked, tapping her coffee cup.

"Just?" Nancy repeated. "I don't mean to be rude, but to me it's very important." She could tell that the reporter still wasn't satisfied, but Holly would have to back off—for now.

The huge jaws gaped open, revealing rows and rows of sharp triangular teeth. Nancy stood mesmerized as the shark brushed against the glass case, snapped its mouth shut, then swam on.

While Annie and Dr. Winston met with the TV crew, the girls got their first glimpse of the underwater world at the aquarium. Jackson Winston had begun their tour with the sharks.

"This exhibit is called the Open Ocean," he explained, as they moved up a spiral ramp, "commonly known as the shark tank."

Nancy was still staring through the glass when another jagged-toothed shark swam by. "That's a sand tiger shark," Jackson explained. "They can grow to be up to eighteen feet long, and they'll eat anything—tin cans, wool overcoats, even bicycle parts."

"Not picky eaters," George commented.

All around them, sharks were on the prowl. Blue light streamed through the tank's water, giving the dimly lit ramp an eerie glow. "I feel as if we're underwater, too," Nancy said.

"That's because we're surrounded by water," Jackson explained. "Right now we're inside the cylinder you saw from outside the building, which houses two ring-shaped tanks. The tank around us is like a giant doughnut—and we're in the center."

Jackson led them up the spiral ramp from which they had different views of the shark tank. "There's another ring-shaped tank above the sharks. It's set up as an Atlantic coral reef, with tropical fish, starfish, sea anemones—that sort of thing."

They paused again to watch a hammerhead shark swim by. Its head was flat and spread out like a hammer, with an eye and a nostril on each side. "Is it true that sharks are man-eaters?" asked George.

"That's a good question for the expert," Jackson said, waving to a young man who was striding up the ramp ahead of them. "Hey, Chris, can you help me out here?"

Nancy leaned back against the railing as Jackson introduced the girls to the young man wearing khaki pants and a royal blue polo shirt with the aquarium's emblem on the pocket. "This is Chris Marconi, our curator of fishes. Also our resident shark expert."

"Not to mention a shark in the dating pool," Chris added, giving Nancy a wink.

"Thanks for the warning," Nancy said, smiling as she studied the man Annie had warned her about.

"Chris is a member of the task force, too." Briefly, Jackson told Chris about Nancy's investigation.

"I see." Chris shoved a mass of unruly black curls out of his blue eyes, then turned to George. "So you have a question about our resident sharks?"

"Are any of them man-eaters?" she asked.

"Hard to say." Chris shrugged. "It's true that some sharks will eat people, if they have a chance. It's also true that some people eat sharks. So I guess it all evens out in the end."

Nancy and George looked at each other and burst out laughing.

"I'm giving the girls a quick tour of the place," said Jackson.

A toothy grin lit Chris's face, and for a moment Nancy was reminded of one of the great white sharks that had just cruised by. "Sounds great," he said, falling in step with them as they continued up the ramp. "Mind if I tag along?"

"Not at all," Nancy said. When they reached the coral reef exhibit, Chris lived up to his "shark" reputation by flirting with Nancy, but she couldn't help being impressed by his knowledge of fish and other marine life. While George and Jackson moved up the ramp, Chris waved Nancy over to the glass.

He pointed out an octopus that was hiding between two rocks, and he reeled off a list of names as the fish went zipping by. "Butterfly fish, angelfish, damselfish . . ."

"Stop!" Nancy said, laughing. "You're making my head spin."

Before Nancy could move, Chris placed his hands on the glass just above her shoulders, cornering her. "You know, Nancy Drew, you have the most amazing blue eyes. Did anyone ever tell you that?"

"My boyfriend tells me that all the time," Nancy answered smoothly. An image of her handsome boyfriend, Ned Nickerson, flashed through Nancy's mind, and her heart skipped a beat. There had been time for only a quick goodbye on the phone the night before she left River Heights, the small city near Chicago where she lived with her father.

"Oh—she's got a boyfriend." Chris swung his arms down and let out a resigned sigh.

"Besides," Nancy added with a smile, "I'm not in your league. I never swim with the sharks."

"Nancy, you're breaking my heart," Chris said, a look of mock anguish on his face. "Can I win you over by buying you lunch?"

"Lunch sounds great," she agreed, "with George and Jackson, that is."

"You drive a tough bargain," Chris said, and his crooked smile made Nancy laugh.

They caught up with George and Jackson outside the coral reef exhibit. "Are you guys ready for some lunch?" Nancy asked. She gave Chris a playful punch in the arm. "Chris is buying."

"Great!" George's brown eyes lit up. "I'm starving."

Chris made a show of looking shocked. "In that case, we're eating in the Pier 4 snack bar."

Leaning over George's shoulder, Jackson showed her where they were on the map. "Here we are—on level four, where the walkway from the ring tanks leads into the main building. Right now we need to go down to the lobby level."

"This building seems to go on forever," George said, craning her neck as they rode down the escalator.

"It *is* huge," Chris agreed. "And there's a separate building, which we call Pier 4." He pointed it out on Nancy's map. "That's where the dolphins and whales are kept. The snack bar is also in that wing."

Nodding, Nancy tried to study the map on the brochure as they rode the escalator, but it was hard to concentrate.

"It must be tough to get through the building with all these crowds," George said.

Chris shrugged. "Fortunately, there are hidden passageways behind the exhibits, as well as fire stairs and elevators."

From level two, Nancy and George got their first glimpse of the wide, octagonal turquoise pool in the lobby of the main building.

"That's got to be one of the biggest swimming pools I've ever seen!" George exclaimed.

Looking down, Nancy agreed. "It takes up most of the lobby."

As Nancy stepped onto the escalator that led

down to the lobby, she saw ribbons of blue light shimmer through the clear water in the pool below. Triangular creatures called rays moved across the pool, rippling and gliding like flying carpets. A waist-high rail separated the pool from the visitors who wandered through the lobby.

Once the group reached the lobby, George and Jackson led the way to Pier 4, passing school groups and mothers pushing strollers.

"So tell me, Ms. Detective," Chris began, "have you uncovered any revealing evidence yet?"

"So far I seem to have more questions than answers," Nancy admitted, "though you can help fill me in." She wouldn't admit that many of her questions involved Chris's involvement with Annie.

"Oh, no!" Chris raised his hands in mock surrender. "Not an interrogation!"

Smiling, Nancy nodded. "Now where did I leave my truth serum?" she asked, pretending to search the pockets of her russet suede skirt.

Chris's blue eyes glimmered as he laughed. "Oh, go on and ask your questions. I'd like to help Annie find this creep, even if she is a snob."

A snob? Nancy hadn't gotten that impression at all, but she decided not to press the matter. One thing was clear: Chris and Annie did not see eye to eye on a lot of things.

They made their way across a sunlit causeway connecting the main building with the smaller building on Pier 4. Talking amiably, Jackson and George walked a few paces ahead of Chris and

Nancy, which gave Nancy a chance to ask Chris some questions.

"How long have you been on the task force?"

"About four or five months."

"Just what do you guys do?"

"At first we had a lot of meetings and handed out a lot of literature. But things started to heat up when people tipped us off about two companies—Paperworks and Mills."

Nancy nodded. "Annie mentioned them. She says they're both dumping waste into the Chesapeake Bay."

"It's very frustrating." Chris pushed his curly black hair out of his eyes. "We have to catch them in the act before we can report them to the authorities. So we're keeping watch with late-night patrols on the bay. It's a drag."

"That does sound frustrating," Nancy agreed.

Chris sighed. "I'd rather take action right now against the companies. If those corporate giants are destroying the environment, they deserve whatever happens to them. But Annie has everyone else convinced to lay low until we have solid proof that they're breaking the law."

Nancy nodded. Annie's plan made sense, although Nancy could understand Chris's impatience.

At the end of the enclosed bridge, they entered Pier 4, and Nancy found herself in a sunny cafeteria. She spotted George and Jackson already in line. "Leave it to George to find the quickest route to food," Nancy said.

Chris laughed. "I'm glad to see that you've

lightened up on the interrogation," he said as they joined the line to the snack bar.

Nancy would have liked to learn more about the task force, but she let the subject drop as they approached the front of the line. "Save us a table," she called out to George and Jackson, who were being handed their food.

George let out a laugh as Jackson put a dish of fries on her tray. "You'll never believe it, Nan," she called back. "They've got french fries shaped like whales!"

Nancy was just about to sit down to a lunch of a hamburger and fries, when she noticed that the wall opposite the snack bar contained a glass window to an aquamarine pool. A moment later, a large gray shape swept by, too quickly for her to make out its details.

"What was that?" she asked, picking up her burger.

Chris glanced over his shoulder, then answered, "One of our beluga whales."

Jackson nodded. "There are a few windows on this floor called viewing stations. You can look directly into the lower half of the pool in the amphitheater."

Judging by the shrieks of delight from the children gathered around the viewing station, Nancy could tell that the whale was a hit.

As soon as the group finished eating, Jackson showed them the rest of the building.

"The focal point of this wing is the amphitheater," Jackson said as he led the girls back up the stairs and pointed to the four sets of double doors at intervals along the corridor. "This is where the dolphins and whales do their stuff." He pushed open a door and motioned them inside. "They're between shows, so we'll just take a quick peek."

Nancy was impressed at the size of the circular theater. Rows and rows of bleachers curved around half of the huge round pool. The other half was surrounded by windows, which allowed natural sunlight to dance along the water's surface.

"Cool!" George exclaimed. "This would make a great swimming pool."

"Except that it's filled with surprises," Chris said, wriggling his dark brows.

"And it's lined in glass. It's like a big glass bowl," Nancy said, walking down the aisle toward the giant pool.

At that moment a whale poked its bulbous head above the surface of the water, let out a cheerful squeal, then dove again.

Chris smiled. "That's Anore."

Glancing across the pool, Nancy saw a narrow platform that jutted into the water, nearly dividing the pool in half.

As she watched, a thin, dark-haired man in a wet suit approached from the side of the pool, hopped onto the platform, and knelt down to stroke the nose of a whale. The group caught his eye, and he waved. "You guys staying for the presentation?"

"Just passing through," Jackson said, tossing off a quick salute. Turning back to the girls, he explained, "That's Doug Chin, our assistant curator in charge of seals and whales. You'll have to catch the show before you leave. These creatures are real crowd-pleasers."

"Do you ever work with the dolphins and whales?" Nancy asked Chris as they headed out of the amphitheater.

"No. As an aquarist, I specialize in fish—the ones with gills. The dolphins, seals, and whales are mammals, so they're cared for by mammalogists. We all try to have a working knowledge of everything that goes on here, though. Annie and Russ Farmer work with the dolphins. Doug and another mammalogist, Megan O'Connor, work with the whales and seals."

"We saw Megan feeding the seals this morning," George added. "It was quite a show."

They retraced their route, then went up to the top level, which housed the tropical rain forest.

The minute Nancy stepped through the door, she felt the hot, humid air and caught the scent of moist earth and vegetation. Palm trees towered in the air, filling the sunny space of the glass rooftop pyramid.

George craned her neck as she stared up, past a rushing waterfall, into the leafy jungle. "You expect to see Tarzan swinging down from one of these trees," she said with a laugh.

Exotic birds fluttered through the dense foliage, their high-pitched calls echoing through the steamy air. Watching the birds dart overhead,

Nancy could see that a crafty person could manage to capture one. There were no cages, nets, or bars.

Chris checked his watch. "I want to show you some fish that are exhibited in their own tanks— electric eels and puffer fish that inflate themselves. Then I have to get back to work. The sharks are due for a feeding."

Nancy, George, and Jackson followed him out of the rain forest and down to level three. They entered a room lined with glass windows looking into individual tanks.

"You'll get a charge out of these babies," Chris said, pointing to a tank containing a snakelike fish. "This guy is commonly called an electric eel, although he's actually related to catfish and carp."

"Do they really produce electricity?" Nancy asked.

Chris nodded. "Enough to disable a cow. But don't worry. You won't find them in the waters of North America."

Nancy stepped aside as a young boy and his mother made their way over to the next window. She watched the boy press his nose to the glass. "Look, Mommy," he said, "these fish are sleeping."

That doesn't sound right, Nancy thought. She walked over to the tank and looked at the spiny fish floating on the surface of the milky water. So far, all of the other tanks and pools at the aquarium had seemed clear and clean, but this one wasn't so appealing.

Her stomach turned as she studied the lifeless bodies of the fish. She was not a marine biologist, but she could see that something was very wrong.

"Chris," she called, motioning him over to the window.

He took a step forward, then gasped. "The porcupine fish! They look like they're dead!"

Chapter

Four

"THEY WERE FINE when I fed them this morning," said Chris, still staring at the tank.

Nancy could tell that he was upset. He strode across the room and yanked open a door marked Employees Only. "I'm going to get to the bottom of this," he said, ducking inside.

Nancy took a step toward the door that Chris had disappeared behind. "I want to see if I can give Chris a hand," she told George and Jackson.

"Mind if I don't join you?" asked George. "I don't think I'd be much help."

"We'll meet you back at my dad's office. Can you find the way?" asked Jackson.

"No problem. I still have this map," Nancy said, pointing to the brochure in her skirt pocket. Then she tugged open the door and stepped inside.

She found herself in a wide corridor with bare concrete walls and floor. As Nancy tried to save her suede pumps by stepping around puddles, she guessed that this area endured a lot of traffic—and a lot of splashing water as fish were removed from their tanks for checkups and treatment.

She found Chris at the top of a short stairway beside a square concrete tank. "There's no doubt about it. These guys are dead," he told her.

Nancy watched as Chris put on gloves to protect his hands from the fish's tiny sharp spikes and dropped the dead fish into a bucket. When he was done, he brought the bucket down to the work table, where he and Nancy studied one of the grayish fish speckled with dark brown spots.

"Can you tell what killed them?" Nancy asked.

Chris shrugged. "Could be a virus, but I've never seen one that disables fish so fast." With a quick look back at the tank, he added, "Fortunately, each of these tanks has its own filtration system. Otherwise, whatever killed these guys could have wiped out hundreds of fish."

She nodded at a tangle of plastic piping that was churning water into the tank. "Sounds like the filtration system is still running, so that doesn't seem to be the problem."

Chris went over to the pump, picked up a clipboard hanging beside the tank, and quickly read the piece of paper on it. "According to this status report, the system was working fine this morning."

He let the clipboard drop, then took a beaker

and a box of labeled bottles from the table and climbed the stairs to the top of the tank. "We can run a few tests on the water right here, but just in case, I'll send a sample to the lab. And our in-house vet will perform autopsies."

"That should help," Nancy murmured. The situation at the aquarium was getting worse by the minute, she thought.

"Do me a favor and bring me that rack of test tubes on the shelf against the wall," Chris said as he dipped the empty beaker into the tank. "I want to test the pH levels."

Nancy picked up the small rack and carried it up to the top of the tank. As she watched Chris work, her eyes began to burn, and she noticed a familiar smell. "Why does this tank smell like a swimming pool?" she asked, thinking aloud. After a pause, an idea struck her. "Could it be—"

"Chlorine," Chris said, holding one test tube up as definitive proof. "Someone added a lethal dose of chlorine to the water in this tank!"

Just then Nancy noticed a white slip of paper wedged between the tank and the filtration system. She reached down and picked it up. The message was no surprise.

"This is no accident," she told Chris. "According to this note, these fish are 'victims of the task force.'"

Later that afternoon, Nancy, Chris, Jackson, and George met Dr. Winston in his office. Nancy and Chris had already filled in the director on the incident with the porcupine fish. At Nancy's suggestion, Dr. Winston agreed to give the aquarium's security force a special alert to watch for any suspicious activity—from either the public or the staff.

Chris pushed up his shirt sleeve and tapped his watch. "I need to look in on a few of my fish friends," he told Nancy, "but I'll see you guys tomorrow. We should have more info from the lab and the vet by then."

"See you in the morning," Nancy called as Chris headed for the door.

Dr. Winston waited until the door closed behind Chris, then said in a lowered voice, "Do you think that Annie is right about Chris? Could he be the one making the threats?"

Nancy frowned. "I'm afraid Chris is one suspect, but he seemed genuinely surprised about those dead fish. It could be any of the aquarium employees. The person who poured chlorine into that fish tank had access to the back room."

Dr. Winston nodded grimly, then picked up a thin sheaf of papers from his desk. "Annie dropped this off for you," he said, handing the papers to Nancy.

She leafed through the three-page roster of task force members. Annie had jotted some notes and placed stars next to the names of key members. "Thanks," Nancy said. "I'll study this tonight."

Dr. Winston turned to Jackson. "Why don't you take these two ladies out and show them around Baltimore? It's almost four o'clock. We're closing in an hour, anyway."

George gave Nancy a hopeful look, and Nancy considered the next step in her investigation. Dr. Winston had already agreed to allow her to examine the personnel files on all the current aquarium employees. The next morning she was planning to interview some of the staff members and find out how people felt about the task force.

In the meantime, it *would* be great to spend some time seeing the city. "I guess a little fresh air might give us a new perspective on the case," Nancy said, grinning.

"Great!" George jumped to her feet. "Where do you want to start?" she asked Jackson as she went over to the coat rack and took down coats.

"How about Fort McHenry?" He pulled on his jacket. "It's just across the harbor, and if we hurry we'll catch the last changing of the guard."

"Sounds good," Nancy said, adding, "We can take our rental car. It's parked in the underground lot of the Lady Baltimore Hotel."

"I don't mind driving," Jackson said as he headed toward the door. "Besides, my car is closer. It's right outside in the employee lot."

Out in the hall, Nancy spotted Chris standing outside a cubicle and talking to someone. She was about to call out a goodbye when the tone of his voice stopped her.

"When are you going to see the light and dump that jerk?" Chris snapped angrily.

"I don't want to discuss it—especially with you," said a stern voice—Annie's voice.

I'll bet he's talking about her boyfriend, Nancy thought.

"You know," Chris added, "you've got a lot of nerve dating him. Especially after those tips we got about Mills. How does he explain that, Annie?"

Mills? Nancy frowned. That was one of the companies accused of polluting the Chesapeake Bay. She wondered how Stuart was connected to the place.

"The task force is investigating Mills," Annie retorted. "If the company is guilty, Stuart would like to know about it, too!"

"I can't believe you'd fall for that!" Chris snapped.

"I don't have to clear my love life with you," Annie added. "Go hit on someone your own speed—and leave me alone!"

Deciding that it was best to pretend she hadn't heard their argument, Nancy kept walking out to meet George and Jackson the parking lot. She couldn't help wondering, though, about the antagonism between Annie and Chris. Was there any foundation to Annie's suspicions of Chris? Or was it simply a matter of bad chemistry?

"Present arms!" shouted a soldier dressed in the garb of a U.S. militiaman of the early 1800s. Three soldiers dressed in similar uniforms swung their muskets off their shoulders and pointed them to the sky. "Fire arms!"

There was a loud boom as the charges exploded. The group was standing in the courtyard of the restored brick fort, and Nancy smiled as George held her hands over her ears to muffle the noise.

After the demonstration, Jackson took them through the museum, where historic flags, military uniforms, weapons, and documents were on display.

"Fort McHenry is probably most famous for its role in the War of 1812," Jackson explained. "The British had landed in Maryland in August of 1814. They had already burned the Capitol and the White House when they began to shell Fort McHenry from the harbor."

"And that battle inspired our national anthem," Nancy said, reading from a brochure.

"That's right." Jackson led them past a display case with shiny sabers, then opened the door so that they could see the exterior of the fort before the sun set.

As she walked along the frozen grass and watched the orange sun set over the gray harbor, Nancy wished that the aquarium was as easy to defend as a fort.

Looking back on that day's incidents, she knew it was time to concentrate her investigation on the *inside*. Most likely, the animals had been killed by someone who had access to them. At least, that had to be true of the porcupine fish. The general public didn't have access to the actual fish tank; visitors observed the fish through a glass panel that made up one side of the tank. And while Chris was removing the dead fish from the tank, Nancy had had an opportunity to question some of the aquarium employees who worked in that area. None of them had noticed strangers wandering behind the scenes.

It was getting dark by the time the threesome climbed back into Jackson's car. They decided to stop for shrimp and crabcakes at a small seafood restaurant at Harbor Place, the bustling complex near the aquarium and the Lady Baltimore Hotel, where the girls were staying.

"This is delicious," George said, taking another bite of a crispy crabcake. "Do you think this seafood came right from the Chesapeake?"

"This time of year, it's probably shipped in from the Gulf of Mexico," Jackson explained. "But the Chesapeake waters are filled with fishing boats in the summer. The truth is, crabs are just one of the reasons we need to protect the waters in our area. All of our wildlife is at risk. That's why Annie started the task force."

Nancy swallowed a spoonful of chowder, then asked, "Has anyone at the aquarium raised any objections to the group?"

"Not that I know of. In fact, most of the curators are members and staunch supporters. There are a few lawyers and university people on the force, too, but the core of the group seems to be aquarium people like Annie and Chris and Russ."

And how do they all get along? Nancy wondered. She had witnessed the tension between Annie and Chris. Nancy would also have to check to see how Annie got along with the others in the group.

41

George took a hot piece of corn bread from a basket on the table. "I wonder if someone at the aquarium has a personal vendetta against Annie."

"That's exactly what I was wondering," Nancy said thoughtfully. It was the first thing she would try to find out in the morning.

The next morning, Nancy sorted through the clothes in her suitcase, tossing aside the shoes she had worn the day before. "Suede is out," she told George. "I must have walked through half a dozen puddles behind those fish tanks." She chose an oversize royal blue shirt with black leggings and high-top sneakers.

"It's an aquarium," George said as she pulled a red sweater on over her blue jeans. "You have to expect a little water."

Downstairs, the girls grabbed a quick breakfast in the hotel coffee shop. Afterward, they pulled on their jackets and headed off along Pratt Street. They walked past the Harbor Place shopping pavilions—two long buildings covered with hundreds of twinkling lights—until they reached the aquarium at the far end of the inner harbor.

Since it was only nine-thirty and the aquarium didn't open to visitors until ten, Nancy and George used their special passes to get into the administrative section, where employees were already bustling around in their cubicles.

Nancy was about to knock on the door of Dr. Winston's office when the door opened and the distraught director nearly barreled into her.

"Oh, Nancy . . . I'm sorry. I was just going to call you, but there's so much to do here, I don't know where to begin," he babbled uneasily.

From the pallor of his face and the strained look in his eyes, Nancy could see that he was upset. "What's wrong?" she asked. "Has another animal been—"

"No," he answered quickly. He gestured for Nancy and George to follow him into his office, where he collapsed into his desk chair. The two girls stood expectantly in front of his desk.

"It's worse than that—much, much worse," Dr. Winston told them.

Clasping his hands over his eyes, he leaned back in his chair and sighed. "I just got a call from the Maryland State Police. Annie is dead."

Chapter

Five

DEAD? Nancy couldn't believe it.

She exchanged a look with George, who seemed to be just as shocked as she was. "That's terrible," George murmured.

"How did it happen?" Nancy asked.

"I'm not sure of the details," Dr. Winston replied sadly. "The police told me that they found her body in the bay near Bodkin Point. Annie owns—or, rather, owned—a small cottage there. They're still searching for her boat. Apparently, she drowned."

After waiting a moment for Dr. Winston to compose himself, Nancy said, "I'd like to drive out to Annie's place and look around."

Dr. Winston nodded. "I'll have Jackson drive you. The cottage is a little hard to find, but we've been there a few times for barbecues."

Dr. Winston summoned his son. A few minutes later Nancy and George were on their way to the parking lot with Jackson. Suddenly, they heard someone shouting after them. "Nancy! Wait up!"

Turning, Nancy spotted Chris dashing out the aquarium door and past the seal pool. By the time he caught up with them, he was out of breath. "Just heard about Annie. Dr. Winston told me you were driving out to her place, and I'd like to go. Someone from the task force should be on hand, especially since Annie was getting those threats."

Chris's blue eyes seemed earnest, but Nancy wondered at his interest in visiting the scene of Annie's death. Chris and Annie hadn't exactly been friends.

"I'm parked in the employee lot," Jackson said, and the group continued on to the car.

As they drove out of Baltimore, the mood in the car was somber. After a few minutes of cruising on Interstate 95 they turned onto a narrow highway and continued south to Bodkin Point. Nancy peered out the window as the tall buildings of the city gave way to the tree-lined streets of suburbs.

As they drove, Nancy thought of the events leading up to Annie's death. There were the anonymous threats, the incidents at the aquarium, Annie's heated argument with Chris, and now this—a tragic drowning. It might be an accident. On the other hand, it could also be the work of someone who was serious about stopping the task force.

"Did you hear anything about those porcupine fish yet?" Nancy asked Chris.

He nodded. "We were right. Someone dumped chlorine—lots of it—into that tank. That's what killed the fish."

Soon the houses were spaced farther apart, and the group passed some marshlands with tall swampgrass and low-lying water. They passed unpaved side roads that twisted down to small waterfront cottages.

"We're getting closer to the water," Chris said, pointing over the dashboard. "You have to turn left onto one of these dirt roads."

Jackson jerked the wheel to avoid a rut in the road. "We turn left at Lenny's Bait and Tackle," he said. "I remember it from the last barbecue Annie invited us to."

They had driven three or four miles when Nancy spotted the weathered wooden sign marking Lenny's. "There it is." The wheels spun as they turned onto the dirt road beside Lenny's ramshackle wooden shack. Nancy noticed that the bait shop backed up to the water, where there was a tiny marina housing a handful of boats.

Slowing the car, Jackson followed a curve in the road. The minute they rounded the bend, Nancy knew they had arrived.

Two Maryland State Police cars and one county police car were parked on the grass in front of the small cedar-sided cottage. A large police van with the words Scuba Team painted on the side panel was parked in the dirt road, along with a handful of other cars. A television news team was on the scene, too, and people were swarming everywhere.

Despite the action on the waterfront, a crowd seemed to be forming around the TV reporters. The camera crew was setting up equipment beside the scuba team's van, and a blond woman, whom Nancy recognized as Holly Payne, was motioning two of the divers to step in front of the camera.

"I guess Holly Payne will have a real story now," Nancy said sadly as they got out of the car.

"Let's watch," George suggested. "We might pick up some useful details."

Jackson and Chris were already edging toward the television crew.

"You guys go ahead," Nancy said, glancing toward the waterfront. "I want to see what's happening down on the beach."

As Nancy wove through the crowd, she saw that the house was cordoned off with police tape. She followed the tape to the side yard, where she came upon two men who seemed to be discussing the case.

Nancy listened in as a tall, uniformed state trooper spoke quietly with a dark-haired, olive-skinned man wearing a well-tailored cashmere coat and leather gloves.

"Our scuba team found the girl early this morning, near Terns Landing," the trooper said, pushing back his wide-brimmed hat. "Looked like a drowning, but we won't know for sure until the medical examiner checks out the body. We'll send you a copy of the report, Detective DePaulo."

DePaulo? Nancy's eyes locked on the Hispanic man in the cashmere coat. This was the Baltimore City detective whom Dr. Winston had mentioned. DePaulo had been investigating the threats against Annie and the aquarium.

Nancy glanced down the frozen lawn to where the land gave way to a small, sandy beach. Two divers in wet suits were standing there, drinking something hot and steaming from cups. A short distance out in the choppy water a dinghy carried two other men from the scuba team along the narrow inlet.

"What about the boyfriend?" asked Detective DePaulo. Getting a closer look at him, Nancy saw that he had deep hazel eyes and sandy brown hair.

The state trooper glanced down at his clipboard. "Stuart Feinstein's the name. He reported her missing at three-forty this morning. The guy was pretty broken up when we finally found the body. Started shouting that she'd been murdered."

"That's him over there." The state trooper added, nodding toward a young man sitting on a cedar picnic bench between the cottage and the sandy beach. He was huddled over, his blond head resting in his hands. Nancy could see that he was shivering, despite the big red parka he wore.

"We're taking him back to headquarters," said

the state trooper. "We'll have him sign a statement there. Then he'll be released—unless we stumble on some new developments in the meantime."

"I'd like a word with him before you take him in," Detective DePaulo said.

The trooper nodded. "No problem."

Nancy watched as the detective went over, brushed off the picnic bench, and sat down beside Annie's boyfriend.

"Look at him sitting there, playing the despondent boyfriend," Chris said bitterly.

Surprised at his tone, Nancy turned to find that Chris, George, and Jackson had joined her. She noticed that Chris's fists were clenched as he scowled at Stuart.

"I don't know. . . ." George shrugged. "He looks pretty upset to me."

"Probably an act," Chris snapped. "He could be the one who cost Annie her life. Who knows—maybe he pushed her off the boat himself."

"That's a serious charge," Nancy said. "Besides, Annie's death might have been an accident."

Chris grinned cynically. "Yeah, sure. Remember yesterday I told you about two companies accused of polluting the bay?"

Nancy nodded. "The Mills Company and Paperworks, Incorporated. You said that the task force was investigating them."

"Right. And one of those companies—Mills—employs Annie's boyfriend, Stuart Feinstein," Chris finished, still glowering at Stuart.

49

No wonder Annie and Chris were arguing last night! Nancy thought. As far as Chris was concerned, Annie was a traitor, dating the enemy.

Glancing back at Stuart Feinstein, Nancy realized he was a likely suspect. Stuart might have gotten involved with Annie just to keep her from investigating Mills. But did the thin, blond man have the nerve to kill Annie Goldwyn when she refused to go easy on the company that employed him?

As Nancy watched, Detective DePaulo backed away from Stuart, then thanked the state trooper. "I'll be in touch with your office if I come up with anything on my end," said Detective DePaulo.

A female officer took Stuart's shoulder and led him into a police car. As he passed by, Nancy could see that Stuart had big blue eyes and high, prominent cheekbones. She had a few questions of her own for Annie's boyfriend, but she realized he would be held up at police headquarters for a while. Instead, she pressed forward against the police barricade and waved at Detective DePaulo.

"Excuse me, Detective," she said. "Are you in charge of this case?"

The attractive detective walked over to Nancy. "Well, that's a matter of opinion. As you can see, we've got officers from the state, county, and coast guard working here. I work for the city, where Ms. Goldwyn reported some threats. But I wouldn't say I'm in charge of the case, Miss . . . ?"

"Drew. Nancy Drew," Nancy offered.

"Nancy Drew . . . yes, Dr. Winston told me he was going to bring in a private detective to work on that matter at the aquarium. So you're the new P.I., huh?"

"Confidentially." Nancy smiled and shook Detective DePaulo's hand. "Dr. Winston has been trying to keep the aquarium's problems from the public, so I'm trying to keep a low profile."

DePaulo nodded. "Things are going to start heating up once that camera crew across the yard gets wind of this whole story."

Glancing back at Holly Payne and the TV crew, Nancy shrugged. "There's no stopping them, but I hope they stick to the facts. At this point, speculation could be very damaging to the aquarium. Do you think that Annie's death is related to the threats she was receiving?" Nancy asked him.

He scratched his chin. "Oh, so I see you're trying to get in on my case."

"Only if it's related to mine," she said.

Detective DePaulo smiled. "Hmm. Well, as a detective, you'll appreciate the fact that I can only speculate at this point. The boyfriend says that he and Annie were out on a little excursion last night on Annie's cruiser, the *Friendly Fin.*"

Had Annie been patrolling for the task force, looking for polluters? Nancy decided not to reveal all her information. "Isn't it a little cold at this time of year to go boating?"

"Exactly what I thought," DePaulo said. "But the boyfriend claims that they were doing some investigating of their own. Says they got an

51

anonymous tip about illegal dumping in the bay. They spotted an idling boat, a twenty-foot cabin cruiser. Saw somebody tossing barrels overboard."

"So they caught them!" Chris exclaimed. "Great! Now we can really nail them." He stepped toward the detective. "Were they from Mills or Paperworks?"

The detective paused, then asked Nancy, "Who is this guy?"

"Chris Marconi," Nancy explained. "Chris is a curator at the aquarium and a member of the Chesapeake Bay Task Force. And these are my friends George Fayne and Jackson Winston."

"I see." Detective DePaulo scratched his chin again as he eyed Chris. "I'm sorry to say, your friends couldn't identify the boat or the people on it."

"Or maybe Stuart doesn't want to admit that they're from Mills," Chris commented.

Nancy realized that he had a point. Stuart could be trying to cover for people he worked with. But the police were still searching Annie's cottage, and the coast guard was still combing the bay. Maybe, by the end of the day, they would have clues to help piece together Annie's death.

"Where did they see the suspicious boat?" Nancy asked the detective.

"According to Stuart, they came across the cabin cruiser not far from here, near an area known as Terns Landing," DePaulo explained, shivering and flipping up the collar on his coat. "As soon as they spotted the illegal activity,

Stuart and Annie returned here. She called the police, and he went to the road to flag the police car down, since this place is in such an isolated spot. When Stuart returned with the cops, Annie and the *Friendly Fin* were gone."

"Have you found the boat?" Nancy asked.

"Not yet." DePaulo looked across the choppy water of the inlet as a small coast guard boat cruised by. "But our scuba team and the coast guard have been searching since dawn. The boat is bound to turn up soon."

Nancy glanced up the road at Lenny's, the bait and tackle shop with the small marina behind it. She was itching to check out the inlet, and the only way to do that was to get a boat.

After thanking the detective, Nancy and the others walked up the dirt road. "This may sound crazy," Nancy said as they reached the paved roadway, "but I think it's time for a boat ride."

"Are you kidding?" George asked, pushing her collar over her ears as a brisk wind blew a tuft of saw grass past them.

"I'm afraid not," Nancy replied. "I'd like to cruise along the bay and check for clues. Do you think we could rent a boat from Lenny's?" she asked, nodding toward the ramshackle cedar-sided hut on the main road.

Chris snapped his fingers. "That's a great idea! And I can get us to Terns Landing—that stretch of land the detective mentioned. I'd like to check it out, but we'll need a boat to do it."

So Chris was familiar with Terns Landing. Suddenly, Nancy wondered how he knew so much about this area—and about Annie's affairs. Although Chris livened things up, she had to remind herself to stay objective. Annie herself had pointed Nancy in Chris's direction. He was still a suspect, and Nancy couldn't let her guard down.

While George and Jackson waited outside, Nancy and Chris went inside the small bait shop. A gum-chewing teenager with slicked-back blond hair agreed to let them use his boat for a small fee. "We don't usually rent out our boats, especially not in the winter. Most people don't want to go out this time of year," he said, cracking his gum.

"We're bird-watchers," Chris improvised, surprising Nancy. "We just want to cruise up to Terns Landing and look for nests."

Shrugging, the boy scribbled out a receipt and handed over the keys. "Take the *Lazy Daze.*"

Outside, Nancy waved the keys in the air victoriously.

"Great!" George called as she and Jackson ran over to the dock.

Passing by a handful of boats covered with royal blue canvas tarps, they climbed into the *Lazy Daze,* a twenty-foot Boston Whaler. An open motorboat, it was small enough to maneuver easily. Chris took the wheel, and the rest of the group found seats as he started the boat and steered it into the inlet.

"Keep your eyes peeled," Nancy shouted above the noise of the engine.

"What're we looking for?" asked Jackson.

Nancy shrugged. That was a good question. The coast guard had probably combed this area already, but Nancy wanted to get a look herself. "Watch for any signs of the *Friendly Fin*—or anything that looks unusual."

The bow of the boat rocked as they moved out of the inlet into a larger neck of the Chesapeake. Shielding her eyes from the sun, Nancy studied the shoreline. There were patches of sand, rocky coves, small weathered docks leading to private launches, and gold patches of tall swamp grass, but no sign of the missing boat. Nothing that looked the least bit suspicious.

Staying low to keep her balance, Nancy joined Chris at the wheel. "We'll go as far as Terns Landing," he told her.

"You know the bay pretty well," she commented. "Have you been to Terns Landing before?"

He nodded. "It's been a hot topic for the task force. We've been arguing with the developer who bought the land—a woman named Lydia Cleveland. She wants to build waterfront condos where some endangered species of birds now live."

As the waterfront whizzed past, Nancy looked for any clues that might give her a better idea of exactly what had happened to Annie. Other than a small coast guard boat that moved past them, Nancy didn't notice anything unusual.

Ten minutes after they had left Lenny's marina, Chris cut the engine and let the boat drift into a slip at a newly built wooden dock that was the only man-made structure on the wild marshland. Glancing along the horizon, Nancy saw that the wetlands gave way to tree-covered hills in some spots.

"That's Terns Landing," Chris said, pointing along the beach. "This strip here, all the way up to that old lighthouse on the point. Three hundred acres of unspoiled land, inhabited by thousands of wild creatures."

Jackson tied the Whaler to the pier, then held the boat steady as George, Nancy, and Chris climbed onto the dock. The four of them walked to the end of the pier, where Chris warned them not to leave the beach area.

"The dunes are filled with the nests and eggs of terns and plover. The plovers are an endangered species," he explained. "If you stay near the waterline, you won't disturb them."

A flock of birds scattered as the group filed onto the beach. "Let's split up and see if there's anything of interest here," Nancy told the others.

"Good idea," George agreed, stretching. "And I could use some exercise. Race you to the point?" she challenged Jackson.

"You're on."

With that, they tore off toward the lighthouse. Nancy followed Chris in the opposite direction. "It's beautiful here," she said as they walked.

"I understand why people want to live on the bay," said Chris. "Though I don't believe an undeveloped spot like this should be sacrificed."

Nancy and Chris walked to the end of the property line without finding anything unusual.

They were on their way back to the boat when Nancy spotted something strange at the dock.

"Look!" she cried, pointing ahead. "There's another boat tied up next to ours."

Chris shielded his eyes with one hand. "Could be the coast guard. Can you see the markings?"

Nancy squinted to read the name painted on the hull of the cabin cruiser. "It says . . ." Her voice trailed off. That was impossible! "It's the *Friendly Fin!*"

Kicking up sand, Nancy ran ahead. She could see that Annie's boat was neatly tied up behind the Whaler. She raced to a halt and looked around. Where was the person who had brought the boat in?

Suddenly the screeching and flapping of birds in the dunes behind Nancy startled her. She turned toward the sound—and gasped.

A bearded man in a hunting cap had sprung from behind the hill of sand. He was holding a shotgun—and the glinting barrel was pointed right at her!

Chapter

Six

NANCY FROZE IN PLACE. He's going to kill me! she thought, swallowing hard.

From the corner of her eye, she saw Chris stop short as he, too, spotted the bearded man.

"You're trespassing here," the gunman growled. "Ms. Cleveland wouldn't like that. And you're riding around in a stolen boat." He moved out of the dunes and stepped closer to Nancy. She couldn't help noticing the glint of the winter sun on the shiny barrel of the gun.

"I didn't steal the *Friendly Fin,*" Nancy said quickly. "But I know that the coast guard has been searching for it all morning."

"I'm not talking about the *Fin,*" the man grumbled. Although it was hard to make out his face beneath his dark beard and red hunting cap, his voice was sharp with quiet anger. "I'm talking about the *Lazy Daze.*"

Nancy glanced back toward the dock. "We rented that boat from Lenny's." She nodded at Chris. "He has the receipt."

Chris cautiously stepped forward, pulling the receipt from his jeans pocket.

The bearded man lowered the gun, and Nancy sighed with relief. "Let me see that," he said, snatching the receipt from Chris and quickly glancing at it. "Who gave you this?"

"A young guy with blond hair," Chris answered.

"That's my son, Tyler," said the bearded man, pushing his cap back on his head. "The kid's supposed to be minding the store, not starting a rental agency."

Suddenly Nancy realized why this man was so upset. The Whaler belonged to *him.* "You must be Lenny," she said. "My name is Nancy Drew, and this is Chris Marconi, a curator from the aquarium in Baltimore and a member of the Chesapeake Bay Task Force. I'm sorry about the mix-up with your boat."

Lenny was still frowning as he returned the receipt to Chris. "Guess that part's square. But you folks are trespassing. This land belongs to a friend of mine, Lydia Cleveland, and she doesn't want anyone on it."

Chris held his hands up in a gesture of peace. "We were just about to leave. No harm done."

Looking back at Annie's boat, Nancy said, "If

you don't mind my asking, why are you driving the *Friendly Fin?"*

"Taking her back to Bodkin Point. Was out clamming with a buddy of mine when we spotted her. She'd run aground. But before I could get the *Fin* back, I spotted the *Lazy Daze* tied up here, on Ms. Cleveland's property." He let the butt of the shotgun rest in the sand. "Needless to say, I was spitting mad."

That's for sure, Nancy thought. At least Lenny had been willing to listen before he used that gun, though.

"For a minute there, I was afraid Detective DePaulo was going to arrest us just for getting him so mixed up," George said, and laughed.

"Yeah," Jackson agreed as he stopped for a red light. "Criminal confusion."

Nancy, George, Jackson, and Chris were driving back to the aquarium after sorting through a mountain of details back at Bodkin Point.

When the *Friendly Fin* and *Lazy Daze* had docked at the marina behind Lenny's, Detective DePaulo had still been at Annie's cottage, supervising the collection of evidence. As soon as Lenny pulled in on Annie's boat, a forensic team had boarded it to collect more evidence.

Nancy smiled. "DePaulo didn't like the fact that we took it upon ourselves to search the inlet. But I think it was the story of the gunpoint encounter with Lenny and the discovery of the *Friendly Fin* that really surprised him."

After he had recovered from his initial reaction, Detective DePaulo had struck a deal with Nancy. She would keep him posted on any significant clues she uncovered, and he would fill her in on the results of the forensics tests.

"Do you think that Lenny had something to do with Annie's disappearance?" George asked Nancy as Jackson pulled into the aquarium parking lot.

"According to the police, Lenny has an alibi that checks out, and it sounds good to me. He threw a surprise party for his wife last night." Nancy climbed out of the back seat and zipped up her jacket. "I think Lenny was just lucky—or unlucky—enough to stumble onto the *Friendly Fin.*"

"It's hard to believe Annie is really gone," Jackson said.

"I know what you mean," George agreed. "I hardly knew her, but I keep expecting to see her bouncing through the halls at the aquarium."

Jackson nodded. "I don't know how Dad is going to run the aquarium without her. He asked me to organize a memorial service at the aquarium. It's planned for Thursday."

"You can count on us to be there," Nancy told him as the foursome entered the aquarium. Since Nancy had spent the morning investigating Annie's death, she hadn't been able to do the research she had planned on doing. It was time to roll up her sleeves and go through the aquarium's personnel files.

Jackson and Chris returned to their duties, and Delores showed Nancy and George to a conference room filled with three stacks of cardboard boxes.

"Wow!" George exclaimed when she saw the cartons. "How many people work in this place?"

"More than two hundred," Nancy said, glancing over a master list. "And we're going to go through each and every file." Ignoring George's groan, she sat down and tugged the lid off the first carton.

"Don't be bashful," Nancy teased. "Dig in!"

Four hours later the girls had gone through most of the cartons and two-thirds of a pizza that Delores had brought back from Harbor Place.

"If I have to read one more résumé, my eyes are going to be permanently crossed." George closed an employee file and stretched.

Using the list of task force members that Annie had supplied, Nancy also had called the key members who did not work in the aquarium. The people she spoke with expressed grave concern over Annie's death, but they were unable to offer any possible explanation. No one had heard from her on the night of her death.

"Okay," Nancy said, adding one last notation to a list she had compiled on a pad of paper. "We've gone through all the employee files, and I've talked to the task force members who don't work here. I'll have to meet with the second in command tomorrow."

"Who's that?" asked George.

Nancy glanced down at the list. "Russell Farmer. He's a mammalogist here at the aquarium."

George nodded. "Maybe he'll have some ideas. After combing through all these files, we haven't come up with any brainstorms."

"Just some unusual tidbits," Nancy agreed, picking up the notepad. "First off, we learned that Chris was dismissed from a New England college. Apparently, Annie isn't the first person he didn't get along with. The file doesn't say why he was kicked out, but he went on to finish his degree at a school in California.

"Second, the only people who were fired in the last six months worked on the cleaning crew, and Annie had no dealings with them."

George rubbed her eyes. "All that work for a handful of tiny leads? Sometimes I wonder why you like being a detective."

Smiling, Nancy continued, "But we learned a few things about the people in Annie's department—the mammalogists. Megan O'Connor, the woman we saw working with the seals, just joined the aquarium nine months ago. And last month Annie was promoted over all the other mammalogists. Someone might have resented her promotion."

"And we know that Chris resented Annie for dating Stuart, who might be doing Mills's dirty work," George added. "But there's a big difference between disapproval and murder."

"I'm afraid murder is exactly what we're talking about here," said a voice from the doorway.

Nancy glanced over at Jonathan Winston. His

gray-streaked hair was disheveled from the wind, and she could tell he had just come in from the cold. He pulled off his coat and joined the girls at the conference table.

"I just spent the afternoon making arrangements to have Annie's body shipped to her parents in Florida. Then I met with the police." Sighing, he smoothed back his hair. "The police say that Annie was murdered. The hair and fiber samples found on the boat indicate that there was a struggle. Not to mention the bruises on Annie's body. I won't get into all the graphic evidence, but Annie was strangled before her body was dumped into the bay."

"Now we know we're dealing with someone desperate enough to commit murder," Nancy said, frowning. "That puts this case into the major leagues."

"I wish we could cancel the party," Dr. Winston said, raking his fingers through his hair. "None of us feels much like celebrating. But I don't want to put off our contributors. We can't keep the aquarium going without their help."

Nancy reached over and squeezed his hand. "Don't cancel the party. Annie wouldn't want that."

"You're right," he said. "I just hope you can find out who did it before someone else gets hurt."

* * *

"This is delicious." George took another bite of baklava, a delicate dessert made of thin pastry, honey, and nuts. "Want to try some?"

Nancy was so preoccupied with the case that she barely heard George. "Um . . . uh . . . No, thanks," she mumbled. Taking a deep breath, Nancy refocused her attention on her friend, who sat across the table of the Harbor Place restaurant where they were finishing a hearty Greek dinner.

"Annie's death really threw you, didn't it, Nan?" George observed gently.

Nancy nodded. "She was so full of life. It makes me more determined than ever to figure this thing out."

"Why don't you give your brain a rest, just for tonight," George suggested. "Look at the bright side. We're having dinner in an interesting city, surrounded by water and blinking lights and cheerful tourists. And we've connected with two great guys."

"That's true," Nancy said. "Chris is full of fun surprises, even if we can't rule him out as a suspect." She rubbed her eyes. "You can't help liking the guy. I just wish he and Annie hadn't been such fierce enemies."

"Jackson has been a big help in showing us around," George added. "He's invited us to a basketball game tomorrow night, and we'll have a chance to meet some of his friends."

"Sounds great," Nancy said with a forced smile. Then she shook her head ruefully. "Sorry,

65

George, my brain doesn't want to take a rest. I don't think I can turn it off."

"Okay, you win. So what's the next step?" George asked.

"Tomorrow we should interview some of the employees at the aquarium. Friday's party will be a disaster if we haven't solved the case by then. The press is making a big deal out of Annie's death."

"Yeah, the place has been crawling with reporters since this morning," George added.

"And if they find out that Annie's murder is linked to problems at the aquarium . . ." Nancy's voice trailed off as she looked out the restaurant's glass wall at shoppers browsing through Harbor Place.

"You're right," George agreed. "That would be a publicity nightmare."

"I can't stop thinking about Annie's boyfriend, Stuart," Nancy said.

"Do you think he could've killed Annie?"

Nancy shrugged. "He was there when Annie disappeared, and he does work for Mills. Maybe he's in on the foul play." Checking her watch, Nancy saw that it was almost eight-thirty. "Let's go back to the hotel," she said, picking up the check from the table. "I'll never be able to sleep without some answers. I want to call Stuart Feinstein and see if he'll answer a few of my questions."

Back at the hotel, Nancy looked up Stuart's number and called. Her heart sank when she got a busy signal.

Over the next two hours, as the girls munched popcorn they had bought at Harbor Place and watched a TV movie, Nancy tried the number dozens of times without success.

"Maybe he took the phone off the hook," George suggested, yawning.

"Maybe," Nancy agreed, crawling into bed and pulling the covers up to her chin. She switched off the lights, then lay in bed, wondering what role, if any, Stuart had played in Annie's death until, at last, she fell asleep.

On Wednesday morning, the girls went to the hotel coffee shop for a breakfast of hot chocolate and fresh-baked rolls, then retrieved their rented car from the hotel garage and headed off. With George navigating, Nancy drove to Stuart Feinstein's address, which she had copied from the phone book.

"There it is," George said as they turned into a cul-de-sac surrounded by scattered three-story brick buildings.

Stuart's apartment was on the first floor of a pale brick building with green shutters.

"I hope he's home," Nancy said, pushing the doorbell. When there was no answer, she rang again. Nancy tapped her foot impatiently and leaned over to look in the front window. There was no sign of life beyond the unmoving curtain. The girls started to turn away when the door swung open.

Nancy was about to speak, but instead her mouth dropped open in surprise as she found herself face-to-face with Detective DePaulo. "We were looking for Stuart Feinstein," she explained, staring past him into the apartment.

"I'm afraid you won't find him here," the detective said. "It looks as if our prime suspect has skipped town."

Chapter

Seven

Stuart—A PRIME SUSPECT?" Nancy said, thinking aloud.

"Does that mean he's going to be arrested?" asked George.

"Just as soon as we find him," DePaulo answered, stepping back into the apartment. "He was told not to leave the area. I'm not going to make the mistake of letting him go again."

Following the detective inside, Nancy glanced over the modern furnishings—a black leather sofa and two saucer-shaped gray chairs.

"Do you have a motive?" Nancy asked.

"Right now we're just guessing that they had an argument that became violent," the detective said, turning to Nancy. "You wouldn't happen to know what they were arguing about?"

69

Nancy told DePaulo about the conflict involving Stuart's employment at Mills. "I'm not sure if it interfered with Stuart's relationship with Annie, but I know of at least one task force member who thinks that Stuart was The Mills Company's hired gun."

"Very interesting," DePaulo said, sliding a gold pen out of his coat pocket.

"Maybe he's at work," Nancy suggested.

"Ahh . . . you run through the possibilities like a true detective," DePaulo said. "However, I just phoned Mills. Mr. Feinstein's boss says that he hasn't spoken to him since yesterday's incident."

"I wonder if he's telling the truth," Nancy said. "He could be covering for Stuart or for Mills itself. After all, the company has been accused of illegal dumping."

"Touché." Detective DePaulo jotted a few notes in a pocket diary as he moved through Stuart's living room.

Nancy picked up an address book that was sitting on a table beside the phone. Looking under F, she found three Feinsteins listed—probably members of his family—but they were out of state.

"I thought of that, too," said Detective DePaulo as she returned the book. "But he has no family in this area."

Pacing through the apartment, Nancy didn't find anything unusual. If Stuart wasn't here or at work, he had to be on the run. Where would he go?

Nancy slid open the door to the bedroom

closet and saw rows of suits, pants, and shirts on hangers. "That's strange," she said aloud.

"Find something?" George asked.

"Just a closet full of clothes," Nancy told her as Detective DePaulo joined them in the bedroom. "If Stuart was really skipping town, wouldn't he pack up all his clothes and belongings?"

"Possibly." DePaulo looked thoughtful. "But maybe the guy is panicked and traveling light."

After they finished searching the apartment, Nancy and George waited on the front lawn while DePaulo carefully locked the door.

Two large shrubs stood under the window of Stuart's living room, just to the left of the front porch. When Nancy noticed that the branch of one bush was broken off, she went closer to examine it.

"Look at this," she said, lifting the broken branch. One part of the bush was flattened, as if someone had fallen on it.

"I guess Feinstein's gardening skills leave something to be desired," DePaulo teased.

George and the detective joined her beside the bushes. Nancy was kneeling on the ground when George plucked a piece of black knit cloth from a branch. "It's a ski mask," George said, holding it up.

Nancy frowned. "I don't know what to make of this, but I'd love to get some answers from Stuart Feinstein."

Detective DePaulo sighed. "It looks as if, for the moment, Stuart Feinstein is leaving us in the dark."

Nancy nodded. In the meantime, she would have to talk to people who could provide some answers, and that meant interviewing Annie's colleagues at the aquarium.

When Nancy and George stepped into the lobby of the aquarium, they noticed a small cluster of visitors gathered around the bright lights and portable equipment of a TV camera crew.

"Looks like Holly Payne is taping another segment," George said as she and Nancy wove through the crowd to get a better look.

"Since the aquarium's opening, millions of visitors have passed through this lobby," Holly intoned, her blue eyes focused on the camera lens.

The girls watched for a moment, then moved away. The reporter's presence reminded Nancy that time was ticking away, and she still hadn't come any closer to solving this crime. The aquarium party was Friday night, and it was already Wednesday morning!

The girls were halfway across the lobby when Chris waved them over to the giant pool in the center of the room.

"You're just in time to see us swim with the rays," Chris said. Dressed in a form-fitting wet suit, he straddled the railing that separated the public from the wide-open turquoise pool.

"Isn't that dangerous?" Nancy asked, staring down into the pool. "Don't they sting people?"

"Only as a defense mechanism," Chris explained. "And though it's painful if you get stung, it's not fatal for humans."

"Still, I think I'd rather watch," Nancy said, glancing down at the pool full of triangular rays.

"Then I'll have to show off for you," Chris teased. "You know, things were a little dull without you two around yesterday afternoon. Where were you hiding?"

"We had to comb through personnel files all afternoon," George explained.

"Ah! Digging up our family skeletons?" Chris wiggled his eyebrows comically. "I hope mine was interesting at least."

"Definitely," Nancy said, deciding to use this chance to find out Chris's explanation of his college dismissal. "I was intrigued by your school records. How did you manage to get kicked out of that New England college?"

Chris's blue eyes widened in surprise. "You really did find some skeletons. If you want to know the truth, I was proud to be dismissed from that stuffy school. I was involved in a movement against a huge chemical company that donated money to the school. We staged a protest on the steps of the administration building, trying to get the school to turn down the funding until the chemical company cleaned up its act."

Smiling, Nancy told him, "I know the end of the story, so I guess the school didn't turn down the donation from the chemical company."

"Instead, they dismissed me and half a dozen

other students. The rest, as they say, is history."
Chris turned as three other divers joined him.
"Got to start the show," he told Nancy and
George. "Catch you later."

"What do you think, Nan?" George asked.
"Do we have time to watch the presentation?"

"Let's watch," Nancy decided. "We may learn
something that will help us."

"And besides," George teased, "how many
chances will you get to see a guy like Chris in a
wet suit?"

"George!" Nancy could feel herself turn red.
"Just because he's cute doesn't mean I'm interested."

"I know, I know. You're totally devoted to
Ned," George added. "But you don't lose points
for looking."

Chris picked up a portable microphone as the
other three divers tucked in the mouthpieces of
their scuba gear and jumped into the tank.

"Ladies and gentlemen," he began, "welcome
to Wings Under Water."

A hush descended on the crowd as people
pressed closer to watch the presentation. Nancy
leaned against the railing and peered down at the
aquamarine pool. Flat and triangular and
smooth as silk, the gray and black rays glided
through the water like dancing kites. "They look
so graceful," she whispered to George.

"This tank is home to three species of rays,"
Chris explained to the audience. "Southern
stingrays, bluntnose stingrays, and cownose rays,

which are found locally in the Chesapeake and Delaware bays."

"How many live in the tank?" asked a curious boy who was visiting with his class.

"We have fifty rays," Chris answered.

Another visitor asked about the danger of rays, and Chris repeated what he had told Nancy, adding, "Rays are not predators of man. This myth was dreamed up by divers who got scared when manta rays swam over them. With wings that span twenty feet, the manta rays created a huge cloud over the divers."

Nancy was so engrossed in Chris's stories and the sight of the graceful rays that she was startled when Jackson touched her on the arm. The minute she saw his troubled gray eyes shaded by the bill of his Orioles cap, she could tell that something was bothering him.

"What is it?" she whispered.

"I need to talk to you but not here." He nodded at the attentive crowd.

"Come on," Nancy said, grabbing George by the arm and cutting through the audience.

They reached the edge of the lobby, but Jackson waved them on to the exit. "It's outside," he said. "At the seal pool."

Glad that she still had her jacket on, Nancy plunged out into the cold winter morning. The threesome raced around the side of the aquarium until the rocky seal pool was in sight.

Nancy saw a familiar figure, a tall, thin redhead, crouched over on the cement platform. She recognized the woman as the mammalogist who had fed the seals the day that she and George had arrived.

When they arrived at the seal pool, Jackson climbed over the wall, then extended his hand to help Nancy and George up. "That's Megan O'Connor," he explained under his breath. "She works with the seals and whales."

Quickly Jackson introduced Nancy and George to the distraught redhead.

As Nancy moved closer, she saw that tears were running down Megan's cheeks, splashing onto a piece of paper that was crumpled in her fingers.

"She's gone—stolen," Megan said, lifting her tear-streaked face to look at Nancy.

"Who?" asked Nancy.

"Asia." Megan held up the note, then sobbed again. "Asia is gone. Someone has stolen our seal pup!"

Chapter

Eight

"A STOLEN SEAL?" George wrinkled her nose in confusion. "How could someone swipe a seal in broad daylight with all these people around?"

Good point, Nancy thought as she looked out at the visitors gathered around the seal pool. Already, people in the crowd were pointing and staring curiously at her, Megan, George, and Jackson. Nancy could only imagine the stir that would be caused if a thief climbed into the pool and made off with a seal pup.

Fortunately, Nancy and the others were standing behind the pool on a cement platform, so the visitors couldn't hear what they were saying.

Nancy stared into the seal pool, searching the rocky nooks and crannies for Asia. She saw Ike, Lady, and nearly a dozen other seals, but there was no sign of the seal pup.

77

Kneeling down beside Megan, Nancy asked, "Are you sure that Asia isn't inside the building? Maybe one of the other mammalogists took her in for an examination—"

Megan's coppery hair flew around her thin face as she shook her head no. "That's what I thought this morning . . . when Asia wasn't in the pool for the ten o'clock feeding. So I went inside and checked with the other mammalogists."

"Don't you have some system to keep track of the animals?" Nancy asked.

"Yes, we do," Megan said. "We're supposed to sign animals out when we take them from their area, but sometimes people forget. I talked to Doug and Russell and a few of the assistants, but no one had seen Asia." Megan picked up a bucket. "Then I found the note in here."

Nancy noticed that the pail was divided into three sections, and each was marked with a seal's name. The sections marked Marmalade and Queenie were empty. The section marked Asia was still filled with halved fish.

"It was tucked in with Asia's breakfast," Megan said as she handed Nancy the note.

Nancy unfolded the wet paper and read the block printed handwriting: " 'Put the task force on hold, and Asia will return.' "

Jackson frowned. "That makes four incidents now, not counting Annie's murder. I wish this creep would cut us some slack."

"That's for sure," George agreed.

Thinking back to the list of task force members, Nancy remembered that Megan's name had been on it. When she asked the slender redhead about her involvement with the group, Megan said, "Sure, I'm a member, but I'm thinking about turning in my resignation. I can't bear to see our animals suffer just because of some political thing."

"But that's the whole point of the task force, isn't it?" George said. "It's designed to protect the animals and the bay."

Megan shrugged. "Doesn't seem to be working, does it? The newspapers say that Annie Goldwyn was murdered. We've got a dead bird, a tank of dead fish, and now a missing seal. If it means saving our seal pup's life, I'm willing to back off."

Nancy could tell that George didn't agree, but she let the point drop when Nancy said, "I don't think it's a good idea to discuss the aquarium's problems in front of this crowd." She turned to Megan and asked, "Is it okay if I meet you in your office this afternoon?"

"That's fine." After wiping the tears from her cheeks, Megan picked up the empty fish buckets and headed inside the building. "I'll see you later."

As Megan climbed over the stone wall, Nancy's eyes followed the low barricade that circled the seal pool. There were no broken-down areas, no holes that Asia could have squeezed through.

Then Nancy turned to Jackson. "I know your

father wants to keep these problems away from the press, but the stolen seal should be reported. I'm going to phone the news in to Detective DePaulo."

"I'll let Dad know," Jackson said.

"In the meantime, I think we need a plan—and some lunch," Nancy said, nodding toward the restaurants across the water at Harbor Place.

Ten minutes later, Nancy, George, and Jackson were settled in at a corner booth in a cozy Mexican restaurant overlooking the inner harbor. As soon as they ordered, Nancy used the pay phone by the door to call Detective DePaulo and tell him about the missing seal pup. He promised to stop over at the aquarium that afternoon to take an official report.

"We have Stuart Feinstein's apartment staked out," DePaulo told Nancy. "We'll grab him if he turns up there."

Nancy wasn't sure that Stuart was the one responsible for all the incidents going on at the aquarium. After all, how could he gain access to the seal pool and the tank of porcupine fish? She mentioned her doubts to Detective DePaulo, and he suggested that Stuart might be working with an aquarium employee. Nancy agreed to mull over his theory. Then she returned to the table.

"So what's the plan for this afternoon?" George asked as she bit into a corn chip.

"I'm going to track down Russ Farmer, the guy who'll take Annie's spot on the task force." Nancy twirled the straw in her glass of soda, thinking. Then she said, "I'd also like to talk to the other mammalogists Annie worked with. Besides Russ, there are Megan O'Connor and Doug Chin."

"They're all on the task force, too, aren't they?" asked Jackson.

Nancy nodded as a waitress served her a steaming chicken fajita. "I'm working my way down the list that Annie gave me. After that, there are three other key members who work at the aquarium, in the rain forest, I think."

"You're in luck," Jackson said, biting into his taco. "They should be returning tomorrow from an aviculturists' convention in Chicago."

"How long have they been out of town?" Nancy asked. If the three curators from the rain forest hadn't been in Baltimore recently, that would certainly rule them out as suspects.

After a moment of thought, Jackson answered, "The convention started last weekend."

"That disqualifies them as suspects," Nancy said, "though I'd still like to speak with them."

"Do you want me to help you interview people?" asked George as she took a bite of her beef burrito.

Nancy shook her head. "If you don't mind, I need you to search for Asia. The seal pup might still be on the premises, hidden away somewhere."

"I'll search every nook and cranny," George promised.

"And speak to the guard at the visitors' entrance," Nancy suggested. "I'd like to know how Asia could be stolen when there's a camera on the seal pool twenty-four hours a day."

"Nancy Drew? Put it there!" the man said, shaking Nancy's hand firmly. "I've heard your name a million times in the past two days!" Russell Farmer's smile was dazzling against his dark skin.

"And I keep hearing yours." Nancy smiled up at the tall man. With a broad, hefty build, he looked more like a linebacker than a marine mammalogist. "Everyone thinks you're going to replace Annie as head of the task force."

Russ leaned against the doorway of his windowed office in Pier 4. Situated at the edge of the giant mammal pool, the small office looked out at the amphitheater. "Well, I'd be proud to fill her shoes. Though her death was a real heartbreak."

He motioned Nancy into the office. "That's her desk over there." He pointed to a small modern desk tucked in the corner below a poster of a dolphin arched over the ocean. "We shared this office. And we were the ones in charge of the dolphins. You work so closely with these animals, sometimes you feel like their parents. I guess you could say Annie and I were ma and pa dolphin."

"You must miss her," Nancy said as she went to Annie's desk and picked up a framed photo. It was a picture of Annie and Stuart, laughing, standing arm in arm in front of the *Friendly Fin*.

Russ sighed. "I miss her, the dolphins miss

her . . . it's a wonder that this place is still running without her."

"Sounds like you and Annie were close," Nancy said, still eyeing the work area.

"Like brother and sister," Russ said, gesturing toward Annie's desk. "Go ahead, look around if you want."

"Thanks." Nancy pulled out the desk chair and sat down as Russ sat back on the desktop.

The bulletin board behind Annie's desk was covered with posters with the slogans Recycle today for a better tomorrow and Keep the Chesapeake clean!

In the drawers Nancy found a box of tissues, an extra uniform, a bottle of hand lotion, and a few other personal items, but nothing that would help in her investigation. "Did she tell you about the threatening notes she was getting?"

Russ nodded. "Yeah, I saw the notes. Now I wish I'd taken them more seriously."

He looked as if he had lost his best friend. Nancy believed that Russ was sincere. "Do you know if anyone else on the task force has received any threats?" she asked him.

"Just Annie. That is, if you don't count what's been happening to the animals around here."

"Are you thinking of disbanding the task force?" Nancy asked.

"No way! Annie would be back to haunt me in a minute if I let this creep intimidate me. I've been in touch with the other members, and most of them agree." He crossed his arms. "If a few people want to bail out, that's fine. But Russ Farmer is in for the duration."

Nancy was impressed by Russ's determination.

"But look at us, cooped up in this tiny room!" Russ jumped up. "Let me show you around."

"I've seen the amphitheater," Nancy told him as they left the office. "It's very impressive." Her voice echoed through the empty amphitheater as they walked along the cement platform surrounding the circular pool.

From close up, Nancy could see that the giant pool was divided into three sections, to keep the whales and dolphins apart. She followed him to the rear section, where a dolphin had its nose poised on the edge.

"That's a girl," Russ said, reaching down to stroke its blue-gray head.

He motioned Nancy over, and she knelt down and touched the dolphin's bottle-shaped nose. "This is Nani," said Russ. "She's one of our oldest dolphins."

At the other end of the pool, they came to a small windowed office identical to Russ's. "This is for the seal and whale people," Russ said, poking his head in the door. "Hello!"

From her place behind a desk, Megan O'Connor glanced over at the doorway. A stout man with red hair and freckles was leaning over her shoulder. "Oh, hi, Nancy," Megan said nervously. "We're just finishing up here. I'll only be a minute."

"I'm giving Nancy a tour," Russ explained. "I'll send her over when we're through."

"Great," Megan said.

Nancy noticed that Megan was on edge, but she supposed that the young woman was probably still upset over Asia's disappearance.

When they were a discreet distance away, Nancy asked, "Who was that man with Megan?"

"Don't know," Russ said, and shrugged. "I've seen him around before. Cousin or boyfriend or something like that."

Russ completed Nancy's tour with a peek at a special area at the end of a long hallway. "This is one place that most visitors don't get a chance to see," he said as they walked into a room with two surgical tables and medical equipment.

"It looks like a giant operating room, except for this pool." Nancy walked over to the turquoise pool in the corner. It was filled with water, but there were no animals swimming in it.

"This is our animal care and research center," Russ said. "That pool has its own filtration system so that we can isolate and care for a sick mammal. Using this facility, we've been able to rescue and rehabilitate stranded mammals."

"How did Annie get along with her co-workers?" Nancy asked as she followed Russ back to his office.

"Everybody loved Annie," he said, then paused. "Well, maybe not everybody. There was a little bad blood between Annie and Megan a few months ago when Annie was promoted.

Megan had hoped that she would be named curator."

A little rivalry? Nancy thought. She would have to ask Megan about that.

"And then there's Chris Marconi," Russ said, rolling his eyes. "That guy is nuts, and he nearly drove Annie crazy, hounding her about her boyfriend and telling her how to run the task force."

"Do you think Chris might have killed Annie?" Nancy asked.

"I don't know," Russ said. "He's stubborn and radical, but I don't know if he would go that far."

Back in Russ's office, Nancy used his phone to call the office of Lydia Cleveland. She was told by a secretary that Ms. Cleveland was in a meeting.

"My father wishes to invest in the bay area," Nancy lied, "and I heard that Ms. Cleveland might have some worthwhile real estate."

That convinced the secretary. By the time Nancy hung up, she had an appointment to meet the developer in the lobby of the Lady Baltimore Hotel that evening.

When Nancy turned away from the phone, Russ was staring at her. "That was some story you concocted!" he said, laughing.

Nancy shrugged. "It got me the appointment."

He was still chuckling as Nancy left and circled the giant pool to reach Megan's office. Her visitor was gone, but Megan was now on the phone.

Nancy waited outside, then wandered down the hall to the animal care complex that Russ had shown her. Walking past the huge operating tables, she wondered if Annie had ever worked with one of the stranded dolphins in this room.

As she stood at the edge of the clear pool, Nancy could see her own reflection. A second later, she tensed as she noticed something in the reflection—an odd flicker of motion behind her. Or was she just imagining it?

She turned to look behind her, but it was too late. The room was plunged into darkness.

"Hello?" Nancy called into the pitch-black room. This might be just a power failure, but she doubted it. Then she heard a sound behind her.

Every nerve in Nancy's body tensed as she listened to the sound of footsteps. There was someone else in this room!

Suddenly she felt a solid object hit her head. At the same time a hand firmly pushed her forward. "Wait, I— Hey!" The push sent her flying off her feet.

A moment later, she was falling, thrashing through the air—and plunging into the pool of water.

Chapter

Nine

ARMS FLAILING, legs kicking, Nancy fought the force of the water. She felt dazed from the knock on the head, and in the pitch-blackness of the water she couldn't see a thing.

Her clothes were like weights, pulling her down. Unable to breathe, Nancy felt a surge of panic. The water seemed to press against her chest until she was desperate for air. She was going to suffocate!

Nancy's hand scraped against a rough surface. What was that? Reaching out again, she realized that it was the side of the pool. Frantically she swam to the surface.

At last, her head pushed up into the air, and she gasped with relief. In a moment she remembered that someone had pushed her into the pool.

Was he or she still lurking in the room—or worse, beside her *in* the pool?

As silently as possible, Nancy swam to the far side of the pool and grabbed the edge. She felt her head, but there didn't seem to be an injury. She listened for signs of another person but heard only the distant clap of footsteps.

"Nancy!" She heard Russ's hearty voice as he charged down the hall.

A moment later, the lights went back on, and Nancy saw Russ by the wall switch near the door. Megan was right behind him. Otherwise, the room was empty. Whoever had pushed Nancy into the pool had fled.

Megan and Russ ran to the edge of the pool.

"Are you all right?" asked Megan.

"I'm fine. Just help me out of here, please." Russ reached down and pulled her out of the pool.

"I had just hung up when I heard you shout," Megan explained. "What happened?"

"Someone decided I should go for a moonlight swim—without the moonlight," Nancy said, wringing out the bottom of her sweater.

Russ and Megan exchanged a confused look. Then Russ shook his head, adding, "Things are getting too creepy around here."

Together they searched the corridor leading to the animal care complex but found no sign of an intruder. Megan put a hand on Nancy's wet shoulder. "Come on. You need to get out of those wet things."

Nancy used the staff ladies' room to change into one of Megan's uniforms. After drying her hair with a towel Megan had given her and hanging up her clothes on the doors of the stalls, Nancy joined Megan in her office. "We have a presentation with the whales in an hour," the woman said. "Until then, I'll be happy to answer your questions. Doug should be along in a minute, too," she added, nodding to the other desk in the cubicle.

"Great." Leaning down, Nancy cuffed the hem of Megan's khaki pants, which were a bit too long. Otherwise, it felt good to be dry again. Megan had even loaned her an old pair of sneakers.

Nancy asked Megan a few questions about the care of the seals and whales, and about the task force. Unfortunately, Megan's answers didn't offer any new insights into Nancy's case.

"I know that you joined the staff this year," Nancy said. "What did you do before that?"

"I was working at an aquarium in Texas," Megan explained. "My husband and I worked in the same department. When our marriage broke up, he stayed on, and I moved back here to be closer to my family. I'm originally from Baltimore."

Trying to be as diplomatic as possible, Nancy said, "I heard there were some problems when Annie was promoted to curator."

At Nancy's words, Megan's face turned bright red. "And I guess you heard that I resented Annie

90

for that promotion," she muttered. "Well, it's true," Megan continued. "I was a little surprised when Annie was made curator. I mean, she had worked here longer, but I had the credentials for the job, and I sure could have used the extra money." Megan looked at Nancy beseechingly. "But I hope you don't think that I would have hurt Annie over that!"

Before Nancy could answer, a voice from the doorway interrupted. "You're not harping on that promotion business again, are you?"

A slim Asian man stood at the door. He was wearing a wet suit, and his dark hair was slicked back with water. "Hi. I'm Doug Chin."

"My name's Nancy Drew." Nancy recognized Doug from her first day at the aquarium, when she had seen him working with one of the beluga whales.

Doug shook Nancy's hand, then plopped down behind his desk. "Megan's been suffering from guilt ever since Annie died. I keep telling her that Annie wasn't killed by a little on-the-job competition."

"Thanks for the insight, Doug," Megan said sarcastically. Obviously uncomfortable, she stood up and went to the door. "If you'll excuse me, I've got to change into my wet suit for the presentation."

After she left, Doug winced. "I'll pay for that remark." He smiled at Nancy. "Megan has been on edge ever since Asia disappeared."

"I'd love to know how our thief managed to

steal away with a seal pup." Nancy frowned. "Will Asia be okay? I mean, does a baby seal need to be near water to survive?"

"Seals can live on dry land," Doug explained. "Because they're mammals, they can stay out of the water indefinitely. As long as Asia is kept cool, she'll be okay. Winter seems to be hanging on forever, so that shouldn't be a problem."

"What about food?" Nancy asked.

"Asia just switched to solid food a week ago," Doug explained. "If she had been stolen two or three weeks earlier, she might have died without her mother. Our thief had impeccable timing."

That's true, Nancy thought. Did that mean the thief was someone inside the aquarium? Someone who knew the seal's habits and routine? It was definitely a possibility.

"I notice that you aren't a member of the task force," she said to Doug.

He nodded. "It's a worthy cause, but I'm too wrapped up in my work here. I've been doing special research with the whales. And now that Annie's gone, I'll be helping Russ with the dolphins for a while. It's good experience, but I feel bad for the animals."

"Why?"

"The dolphins loved Annie," Russ explained. "It's really sad. Russ and I can see the change in their behavior. They miss their trainer, and I don't know how to tell them that she's never coming back."

* * *

"I'm glad you're okay. If that creep had had more time, you might have been seriously hurt," George told Nancy as she stabbed a fork into a slice of chocolate cake at the hotel restaurant.

Nancy had just finished filling George in on her afternoon. After speaking with the mammalogists, Nancy had questioned a dozen more employees. Over and over, people mentioned the same names: Mills and Paperworks.

"I know," Nancy said. "I guess I'm lucky that I just got to go for a swim."

George laughed. "I have to admit that I was tempted to jump into a few pools while I was searching for Asia. The warm, tropical water seems tempting after all this wintry weather."

"Too bad you couldn't find her," said Nancy.

"I'll say. I checked every fish tank, every closet. I even looked in the walk-in refrigerators. No seal pup. But I did learn something interesting from the security guard. You were right about that closed-circuit TV. On Tuesday night, the monitor showing the seal pool went black."

"What?" Nancy brightened at the clue. "Do you think someone disconnected it?"

"The guard thought it was broken," George explained. "He went out to check the seal pool, and everything seemed to be fine. But the next morning, when the technicians came to fix the camera, they found black tape stuck over the lens—the lens focused on the seal pool."

"So the thief knows the security system," Nancy said. "One of the employees must have stolen the seal pup that night."

George nodded. "He probably waited until the aquarium was closed. If it was dark, the thief could have gotten away unnoticed."

"Dragging an eighty-pound seal behind him?" Nancy asked dubiously.

"I can hear that detective mind clicking away." George smiled. "What are you thinking, Nan?"

"That the incidents at the aquarium are being staged by someone on the inside," Nancy explained. "I still don't know of any employee with enough of a motive, though. It's clear that Annie and Chris didn't get along, but that doesn't tell us why Chris would sabotage the task force."

"Chris is so much fun, I keep forgetting that he's a suspect," George said, wrinkling her nose.

Then Nancy told George what she had learned about Megan. "She was jealous over Annie's promotion, but that's no reason to commit murder."

"Besides," George pointed out, "did you see how upset she was over Asia's disappearance?"

Nancy nodded. "She's a bundle of nerves."

"So where does that leave the case?"

Nancy shrugged. "Detective DePaulo suggested that someone at the aquarium could be working with one of the task force's enemies. That's one reason I'm meeting with that developer, Lydia Cleveland, tonight. And tomorrow morning, you and I are going to check out those two companies everyone keeps talking about."

"Mills and Paperworks?"

Nancy nodded.

"I wish you'd cancel your appointment with that woman and come to the game with us tonight," George said. Jackson and a group of his friends had invited the girls to a pro basketball game.

"Are you kidding?" Nancy teased. "My rich real-estate investor dad would never forgive me."

"What a ruse!" George shook her head. "I hope you can get the information you need before that woman figures out that you're a detective instead of a debutante with a superrich father."

Forty minutes later, Nancy rode the elevator back down to the lobby. She was dressed in a black knit jumpsuit. She was walking by the lobby desk when the hotel clerk stopped her. "Miss Drew?" the woman called. "I have a message for you. Someone phoned this in a few minutes ago."

Nancy took the slip of paper from the clerk and read it: Want to know who killed Annie Goldwyn? Be in the rain forest—9 P.M. tonight.

Nancy read the message a second time. The idea of meeting a stranger in the aquarium's rain forest at night made her shiver. This was not an appealing invitation. She would have to go it alone, too, since George was on her way to the game.

She knew there was a strong possibility that this was a trap. Still, she had to check it out. She would just have to be very careful.

In the meantime, Nancy had a few questions for Lydia Cleveland. She hoped she looked the part she was trying to play. Taking a deep breath, she checked out the people waiting in the hotel lobby.

After ruling out a young couple and three businessmen in suits, Nancy spotted a petite, smartly dressed woman with silver hair held back with a silk headband.

Nancy approached the woman. "Ms. Cleveland?"

"Yes, I'm Lydia Cleveland." The woman smiled as she shook Nancy's hand. "And you must be Nancy Drew." The woman sat back and gave Nancy a critical glance. "I'm afraid the message from my secretary was vague, but your name is familiar. Tell me, are you one of the Atlanta Drews?"

Nancy suppressed a laugh. "No, I'm from outside Chicago," she said, trying to keep her answer general. "My father is interested in making some investments in the bay area, but we've heard a few rumors of problems."

Lydia Cleveland nodded. "Every developer deals with problems. However, I've overcome them in the new complexes we've built down in Annapolis and right here in Baltimore. If you're interested—"

"The rumors were about political problems." Looking Ms. Cleveland in the eye, Nancy said, "We've heard that environmentalists were fighting the development of some areas of the Chesapeake Bay—like your plot at Terns Landing?"

Lydia's smile seemed forced. "Oh, that piece of land has been a thorn in my side. I went so far as to draw up plans for condos at the site, but some group fought us."

That group was Annie's task force! Nancy thought.

"Fortunately, that land won't be a problem much longer," the real-estate developer said firmly.

Lydia seemed awfully sure of that, Nancy thought. Was it because she herself was behind the threats to stop the task force?

"Now I remember where I heard your name," Lydia added sharply, her gray eyes narrowing. "Lenny Miller called me and said you were trespassing on my land, along with a bunch of those radicals from the aquarium."

Oops! Nancy hadn't anticipated that word of her little visit to Terns Landing would get to Lydia Cleveland so quickly.

It was time to drop the charade. "Annie Goldwyn was found dead not far from your land," Nancy stated firmly. "Did you think you could go ahead and build your condos once the head of the task force was out of the picture?"

"No!" Lydia Cleveland seemed genuinely horrified. Indignant, she rose to her feet. "And I resent the implication. I'm a businessperson, Miss Drew. I do not break the law. And I do not have people murdered!" With that, Lydia Cleveland swept out of the hotel lobby.

Nancy mulled over what had happened as she returned to her room to change into jeans and a cotton sweater for her meeting in the rain forest.

Lydia Cleveland had seemed shocked when

Nancy brought up Annie's death, but the developer had admitted that she had plans for Terns Landing. What had she said? *That land won't be a problem much longer.*

By the time Nancy walked through the private entrance of the aquarium, it was already 8:50. She signed in for the night watchman, then used her key to get into the main lobby of the building.

An eerie stillness filled the air. Nancy could see that the escalators had been shut down for the night, so she tried the elevator. It whirred to life as she pushed the button. A moment later, she was in the car, riding up to level five, where the tropical rain forest was located.

Nancy reminded herself that this meeting could be a trap. Even so, she was sure she would be meeting an aquarium employee. Someone from the outside would have no way to get into the rain forest at night, when the building was closed to the public. But who could it be—Russ, Megan, Chris, Doug? Or someone she hadn't even met?

Nancy patted her rear jeans pocket, which held her Swiss army knife. She had brought it at the last minute.

In a matter of moments, the elevator door opened, and she was on level five. She stepped out of the elevator and checked her watch. Perfect timing. It was two minutes before nine.

The heavy door to the rain forest was unlocked. Slipping her key back into her pocket, she tugged open the door and entered the misty jungle.

The rain forest was much darker and noisier than Nancy remembered. The airy space, so alive with visitors and sunlight by day, now belonged to the wild animals who cackled and cooed in the dark. Moonlight filtered in through the glass roof, casting eerie shadows along the path.

Thinking back on high school biology, Nancy remembered that most jungle creatures were nocturnal. Surrounded by chirping birds, croaking frogs, and scampering lizards, she could see firsthand how the animals lived at night.

Nancy moved warily along the path as her eyes adjusted to the dim, moonlit surroundings. She caught a glimpse of a quaint wooden bridge on the path just ahead of her. Then the light faded as clouds passed in front of the moon.

Pausing, Nancy listened intently. The cackling birds and the rustling palm fronds had a regular rhythm, almost like a song. The only problem was, there were no human sounds.

Where was the person who had told her to be there?

At last, the moonlight grew stronger again, and Nancy continued walking toward the bridge, which arched over a narrow stream. As she leaned over the railing and peered at the dark water rushing under the bridge, she wondered what was holding up her contact. It was already ten after nine, and there was no sign of another person in the rain forest.

The stream below had been created by a waterfall that cascaded over a man-made cliff, which Nancy could just barely make out more than a dozen yards away. What kind of wildlife lived in the stream? she wondered, studying the churning water. Frogs? Tropical fish? Killer piranhas?

Not wanting to dwell on gruesome possibilities, Nancy turned away from the water and walked along the bridge. She had just reached the end, where the wood gave way to the asphalt path, when the moonlight disappeared once again. Moving ahead in the darkness, Nancy stepped off the wooden planking and onto the path.

At the same moment, the moonlight returned, and Nancy's eyes fixed on a dark, patterned circle beneath her feet. Her senses told her to step back, but it was too late.

Nancy gasped as the webbed pattern rose around her, wrapping her in its grip.

It was a net! Nancy felt herself being lifted through the air. Her knees came up to her chest as she collapsed inside the swinging net.

The trap had been sprung!

The net was still swinging as Nancy looked down at the stream below her. She was tangled in a net, dangling in the air twenty feet above a brook full of jungle creatures!

Chapter

Ten

SLIPPING HER FINGERS through the loose weave of the net, Nancy held on and forced herself to think rationally.

The security guard was downstairs. Was one of his monitors tuned in on the rain forest? If so, could he see her there in the dark?

There was a chance someone else was working late. Hadn't the curators stressed that they were on call twenty-four hours a day?

But she also knew that the three curators in charge of the rain forest were out of town at a convention. And she hadn't run across anyone else working late on level five.

Still, it wouldn't hurt to try to roust anyone who might be passing by. "Help!" she shouted. "Is anyone out there? Can you hear me?"

Birds flapped and shrieked around her, upset by the noise. Otherwise there was no response.

As she hung in the air, Nancy considered another option. The net between her fingers felt as if it was made of nylon. She could use her Swiss army knife to cut through it. But what then?

The churning stream raced by twenty feet below her. She couldn't jump—it was too far down. Also, she couldn't be sure that the aquarium's piranhas didn't live there.

Then she had an idea. The bridge was only about ten feet down, but it was off to her right. She wasn't sure she could jump onto it from the net.

Deciding to try anyway, Nancy squirmed in the net as she pulled out the knife and opened it. The sharp blade sliced through the net easily, and in a minute she had cut a hole large enough to slip through.

Here goes! Nancy linked her fingers through the mesh of the net and closed her hands, making sure that she had a good grip. Then she pushed her feet through the hole and let her body slide free.

Suspended in the air, holding on tightly to the net, she kicked out hard. Soon she had the momentum she needed. She swung back and forth like a pendulum, out over the water, then over the bridge. Her feet swept near the railing of the bridge as she passed over it, but she couldn't touch the rail.

Arching her back, she kicked out even harder. Swinging toward the bridge once again, she realized it was now or never.

Taking a deep breath, Nancy aimed her feet toward the walkway of the bridge and let go of the net. She leapt through the air, arched over the railing, and landed in a heap on the bridge.

With a sigh of relief, Nancy stood up, brushed off her jeans, and raced through the rain forest. She ran along the path, flung open the door— and ran smack into the broad chest of Chris Marconi!

"What are you doing here?" he asked.

Chris was still a suspect. In fact, he could have been the person who had set the trap! "What brings *you* up here?" Nancy countered.

An embarrassed look crossed Chris's handsome face. "I was working late, and sometimes I like to come up here to think."

When Nancy eyed him dubiously, he shrugged, adding, "Don't tell anyone. I wouldn't want people to think I'm one of those sensitive types."

Nancy was still considering his explanation when Chris asked her why she was so shaken up. She decided there was no harm in telling the truth.

Chris's blue eyes narrowed. "Who'd want to string you up in the rain forest?"

"Someone trying to scare me off this case." Nancy watched to see if he reacted to that, but Chris seemed unfazed.

"It may be scary, but it's not dangerous in

there. I mean, there's a pack of killer piranhas, but they're confined in an inaccessible tank. Not even *you* could stumble into that one."

Nancy grimaced. "So you heard about my little swim in the animal care complex?"

"It's the talk of the aquarium," he said, giving her a devilish wink. "I'm just sorry I missed it."

Nancy changed the subject. She needed to know if Chris had a valid reason for being there that evening. As casually as she could, she asked, "So you're working late tonight?"

"I've got a sick shark on my hands. Come on—I'll introduce you."

Nancy hesitated a moment. She wanted to find out who had caught her in the trap. But she couldn't go back into the rain forest alone, in case someone was still waiting. And she couldn't ask Chris to go with her, in case he was the person responsible. At least, she thought, if Chris *was* the person responsible, he wouldn't make another attempt that night. Also, if she went with him, she could find out if he was telling the truth about the sick shark. "Okay," she said. "Let's go."

They walked over to the cylinder housing the ring tanks and took the stairs down to the first level. Chris took Nancy into a room behind the shark exhibit. There he showed her the shark he had been nursing, which swam sluggishly through the tank.

Chris had some things to finish up, and Nancy was anxious to talk to the guard. She said good night to Chris, then went down to the guard's station. She told him what had happened in the rain forest. The guard was distressed. He told her that he hadn't noticed anything unusual on the monitor, but he promised her that he would cut down the net as soon as he was relieved so that she could examine it. She hoped to be able to find out who in the aquarium might use a large, nylon net.

When George returned from the game, Nancy was sitting in bed, trying unsuccessfully to read. She couldn't concentrate—she kept thinking about Chris.

"Do you think he was the one who lured you into the rain forest?" George asked when she heard Nancy's story.

"I hope not," Nancy admitted. "I can't help liking him. And he really does have a sick shark in isolation. I saw it myself." Nancy paused before adding, "But I can't rule him out as a suspect."

George sat on her bed and pulled off her sneakers. "If you ask me, there are too many suspects—and tomorrow is Thursday! Don't forget, Annie's memorial service is at noon."

"And then there's the big party on Friday night," Nancy pointed out.

George nodded. "Jackson says his father is panicked. He's held the press off so far, but there won't be any way to avoid their embarrassing questions at Friday's party."

Nancy stretched out and put aside her book. "I've got to solve this case before that party!"

* * *

"I'm sorry, ladies, but there's no one here who can handle your questions today," the harried receptionist told Nancy and George.

Right after breakfast Thursday morning, they had driven to Mills, located in the heart of Baltimore's business district. The company's headquarters was abuzz with activity and an undercurrent of alarm.

The receptionist's phone rang repeatedly, and Nancy and George heard a few passing employees gossiping about Stuart Feinstein.

Deciding on another approach, Nancy smiled sweetly and asked the receptionist, "How about Stuart Feinstein? Is *he* in today?"

"Of course not!" The woman regarded them suspiciously. "Are you reporters?"

"No." Nancy held up her hands in a defensive gesture. "We're working on a paper for school."

"Thank goodness." The receptionist glanced down the hall warily. "If someone hears me spouting off to a reporter, I'll lose my job. Things have been crazy here ever since that girl drowned. Between the reporters, cameras, and police, my bosses are tearing their hair out."

"Are they afraid of bad press?" George asked.

"Of course," the woman confided. "It would look terrible for the company if Stuart Feinstein was actually spying on Mills! Monitoring our recycling program on his own! One of our own employees! Chances are, if he ever shows his face here again, he'll be fired on the spot."

Nancy and George mulled over Stuart's situation as they drove through the streets of Baltimore toward the Paperworks factory. "If Stuart killed Annie to get her off the trail of Mills, his plan backfired," Nancy said. "The press is hounding the company, and now that Stuart is under suspicion, Mills has abandoned him."

"On the other hand," George pointed out, "if Stuart is innocent, he's in a real bind now."

"You're right," Nancy said. "He's lost his girlfriend and his job. And he could be on the run, hiding out—or even dead."

Pulling the car into the parking lot outside the waterfront factory of Paperworks, Nancy added, "I wish I could find Stuart. He's the key to this case, and one of the prime suspects."

Inside the massive Paperworks building, the girls were asked to wait. "Our public relations director will be with you in a moment," the receptionist said, peering over his reading glasses.

Nancy and George sat in the empty waiting area. After a few minutes of leafing through magazines, Nancy became impatient. Noticing a water fountain in a hallway off the waiting room, she told George, "I'll be right back."

Down the hall, Nancy took a long drink, then paused as she spotted a doorway marked Employees Only. This was her chance to get the behind-the-scenes look that she wanted, not some speech from a smooth public relations person.

Without hesitating, Nancy pushed open the door and ducked inside. She found herself standing in another corridor, and she could hear the thrum of heavy machinery. Nancy moved down the hall to a pair of heavy doors. She pushed one door open and poked her head inside.

Even though her view was blocked by a frosted glass partition a few feet from the door, Nancy could tell that the machinery was in this huge chamber. The noise was deafening, and a familiar odor burned her nostrils. It reminded her of laundry detergent—the smell of bleach.

"Hey, what's going on?"

Nancy blinked as a stout man wearing goggles and blue coveralls came barreling toward her. Nancy backed out of the room into the hall. A second later, the door flew open, and the angry man stood before her.

"You can't go in there without protective gear," he said, pulling off his goggles to reveal a wide face splattered with freckles. "Didn't you see the sign?"

"Guess I missed it," Nancy said apologetically, studying the man's face. He had short-cropped red hair and a no-nonsense attitude. Something about him seemed familiar. The nametag on his lab coat said Daniel Cribbins. Nancy mulled the name over, but it didn't ring a bell.

She decided to risk asking him a question. "It smells like bleach in there. Is something being cleaned?"

"That's chlorine," Cribbins told her, pulling his goggles over his face again. "That's what we use to bleach the paper pulp. Now, if you'll excuse me, I've got to get back to work."

Chlorine! The word echoed through Nancy's head as she walked back down the corridor. That was the chemical that killed the porcupine fish!

Nancy knew that anyone could buy chlorine in a swimming pool supply store, but she hadn't realized that it would be easily accessible to someone who worked in a paper factory.

She was about to enter the reception area when she noticed a familiar woman sitting on the couch, leafing through a magazine. The shiny silver hair and petite figure belonged to the developer Lydia Cleveland.

Lingering beyond the doorway, Nancy observed a well-dressed man emerge from the opposite hallway. "Lydia!" he gushed. "So sorry to keep you waiting. If you'll follow me, I believe we're ready to sign those papers."

As soon as they disappeared down the hall, Nancy rushed into the reception area and squeezed in next to George. "What in the world is Lydia Cleveland doing here?" she whispered.

George's eyes were bright with excitement. "I heard the receptionist talking to her. Apparently, Ms. Cleveland has offered to sell Paperworks a huge parcel of waterfront land at Terns Landing."

"Terns Landing!" Nancy whispered hoarsely.

"Paperworks plans to use the land to build another factory," George added.

Twenty minutes later, Nancy and George left the Paperworks building and walked to the car. As Nancy had expected, the public relations director gave them the standard, boring spiel. On the other hand, Nancy and George had picked up some valuable information.

"Now I understand what Lydia was talking about last night when she implied that Terns Landing would no longer be her problem," Nancy said. Then she told George what she had found behind the scenes. "I was chased away by a burly man named Cribbins," she added. "He looked familiar. Do you remember meeting anyone by that name?"

George shook her head.

"Nancy Drew!" someone called when the girls were halfway across the parking lot. Nancy spun around to find Detective DePaulo stepping out of an unmarked car and buttoning his cashmere coat.

He closed the car door and joined Nancy and George. "I hope you're leaving town soon," he said with a wry grin, "because you're ruining my case. Every time I approach a suspect or a witness for a statement, I learn that you've already grilled him." The detective grinned. "I'm impressed."

"Well, I suspect that you got to Lydia Cleveland long before I did," Nancy replied. "I just mentioned Annie's name, and she went running out the door."

DePaulo's hazel eyes twinkled. "Maybe I did beat you on that one."

Nancy told him what she had just learned, about Lydia Cleveland selling the land to Paperworks.

"No kidding?" Detective DePaulo seemed surprised. "That's big money for her. I wonder if she'd kill someone who might stand in the way. I must say, ladies, you've gotten pretty far on this case—and you don't even have badges!"

When they returned to the aquarium, the girls went to Jonathan Winston's office to give him an update on the case. "It sounds like you're making progress," Dr. Winston agreed. "And not a moment too soon." He picked up a stack of message slips from his desk and waved them in the air. "These are all calls from local reporters. I can't put off the press much longer."

"I'll do my best to clear everything up before the party," Nancy promised. "But whether it's Mills, Lydia Cleveland, or Paperworks threatening the task force and the aquarium, I don't think they're working alone." Frowning, she explained, "I'm fairly sure that one of your employees is involved."

"Is it Chris Marconi?" Dr. Winston asked.

"I'm not sure," Nancy admitted.

After agreeing to meet again before the party, Nancy and George got up to leave. "Where to now?" George asked when they were outside.

"I want to find that guard who said he'd cut down the net for me. I'd like to take a look at it."

"Jackson always seems to know where everyone is," George observed. "We can find him by the shark tank right now."

"You're keeping close tabs on old Jackson, huh?" Nancy teased.

George blushed slightly. "It's not like that, Nan. But he is nice, isn't he?"

When they arrived at the bottom of the circular ramp that twisted around the shark tank, Nancy saw Jackson talking with one of the other interns.

"Hey!" he called. "You're just in time to watch Chris take a dive in the shark tank." Jackson explained that the shark that was in isolation the night before had been placed back in the Open Ocean exhibit. "But the area's been temporarily closed to the public while Chris dives in to check on the shark's progress and give him some medication."

"There he is!" George pointed to the tank.

Chris swam into view, wearing a black wet suit. He waved at the group.

"Look at that thing!" said George, indicating a long fish that was trailing Chris. "It must be five feet long."

"That's a barracuda," Jackson explained. "It's not a shark, but it's a feisty fish."

As Chris turned to look behind a group of rocks, Nancy noticed a fluorescent yellow ring hanging from the back of his air tank.

"That's strange," she murmured aloud. "I've gone on dives before, but I don't remember that ring as part of the diving gear."

The barracuda had noticed the bright ring, too. The huge silver-and-blue fish still lingered behind Chris, darting behind his back, nosing the ring. But Chris didn't seem to be aware of the barracuda behind him.

"That fish is beginning to go wild," Nancy

said. She tapped on the glass, trying to warn Chris, but he couldn't hear her.

As Chris moved, the ring wiggled in the water, and the barracuda started to snap at it with its sharp teeth. By now Nancy was waving frantically, but Chris didn't notice.

"He doesn't even know the barracuda is behind him," said Jackson.

"Oh, no!" George gasped.

Nancy watched in horror as the barracuda lunged after the ring. It missed the ring, but its sharp teeth cut right through Chris's wet suit and into the skin of his shoulder.

A moment later, a cloud of blood blossomed in the water.

A burst of bubbles rose from Chris's mouthpiece as the shock hit him. Beneath his mask, Nancy could see the horrified look in his eyes as he realized he was being attacked by a barracuda!

Chapter

Eleven

"WE HAVE TO HELP HIM!" Nancy ran up the ramp, searching for a door that would give her access to the tank.

"Up here," Jackson shouted, racing ahead and tugging open a door that blended in with the gray wall surrounding it.

Running right on his heels, Nancy dashed into a room cluttered with small fish tanks and buckets. She nearly slipped in a puddle on the slick concrete floor. "How do we get to the tank?" she gasped.

"It's back here," Jackson called, starting up a short staircase. "But watch your step. The catwalk is narrow, and it juts out directly over the shark tank."

Nancy could see what he meant. The narrow

bridge stretched just a few feet above the gurgling water of the shark tank.

"Where's Chris?" she shouted.

Jackson leaned over the water, searching until at last he shouted, "I see him!"

They shuffled ahead, and Nancy winced as she spied the red mist of blood in the water. A moment later she saw Chris's hand reaching up toward the catwalk.

Rushing forward, Nancy and Jackson knelt down and reached into the water below. Jackson's fingers closed around Chris's wrist, and he managed to hoist Chris up so that he could grab the wooden bridge.

A moment later, both Nancy and Jackson pulled Chris out of the water. Chris pushed back his diving mask, then collapsed on the catwalk. Jackson took a clean handkerchief from his pants pocket and pressed it against the cut on Chris's shoulder.

"How do you feel?" Nancy asked.

"I'm okay," Chris insisted, pulling off his oxygen tank and easing it onto the catwalk. "He just nipped my shoulder."

"The cut doesn't look too bad," Jackson said, "but we'll have the nurse look at it to be on the safe side."

"I'm more shocked than hurt," Chris admitted. "I don't know what possessed the barracuda to go after me. He's a playful fish, but he's never caused me trouble before."

"He was going after this ring on your tank,"

115

Nancy said, pointing to the bright yellow ring attached to Chris's diving gear.

Chris stared at the ring. "No wonder he attacked me. He thought I was taunting him! Barracudas can't resist striking at bright, moving objects." Furious, he slammed his hand down on the wooden catwalk.

"Do you have any idea how the ring got on your air tank?" Nancy asked.

"You're the detective—you tell me!" Chris said, wincing from the pain in his shoulder.

"Whoa! Hold on a minute," Jackson intervened. "I'm only an intern, but I know the rules for diving. Did you check out that equipment before you put it on, Chris?"

"Of course I did," Chris said. "I looked it over in the food prep room this morning. But someone must have tampered with it while I was moving the shark back into the tank."

Nancy's mind clicked away. Had Annie's killer tried to strike again?

When the aquarium's nurse arrived to examine Chris's wound, Nancy and Jackson surveyed the food prep room where Chris had left his diving equipment. They didn't see anything unusual.

Nancy tried to narrow down the list of people who had access to the equipment, but while visitors weren't permitted in the prep area, any number of aquarium workers could have attached the ring to Chris's gear.

"We have an open-door policy here," Jackson explained. "All of the two hundred people who work here are free to come and go through any section of the building."

Nancy felt frustrated. If something didn't break soon, the aquarium's open-door policy was going to allow the killer to slip away scot-free!

"None of us here will ever forget Annie Goldwyn," Jonathan Winston said, addressing the crowd that had gathered in Annie's honor.

The meeting room, just off the main lobby, was filled with teary-eyed employees. Dr. Winston stood at a podium flanked by flower arrangements and candles lit in Annie's memory. One wreath of blue carnations was fashioned in the shape of a leaping dolphin.

From her seat in the back row, Nancy studied the people in the room, most of them familiar from her days of investigation there. She shivered at the realization that one of the mourners in the room was probably involved in Annie's death.

Nancy considered the suspects.

Chris Marconi sat in front of Nancy, clasping and unclasping his hands tensely as Dr. Winston spoke. Chris had been a suspect until his close call that morning. Now that someone had tried to turn Chris into barracuda bait, Nancy was almost positive that he wasn't the person threatening the task force. Luckily, his wound wasn't serious. The nurse had bandaged it and pronounced him fit to go back to work.

Nancy glanced over at Megan O'Connor. The young redhead admitted that she resented Annie for her promotion, yet that alone was a weak motive for murder. Not to mention the fact that Megan had seemed genuinely upset when Asia had disappeared. And Megan couldn't have been the person who pushed Nancy into the pool. Megan and Russ had heard Nancy's shout at the same time.

Who was the rat inside the aquarium? Examining the net earlier that day had told her nothing. Anyone in the aquarium could have gotten one. Nancy ran down the list of other possible suspects: Russ Farmer, Doug Chin, Jackson Winston, Delores, and Jonathan Winston. Nothing pointed to any of them. She sighed. At the moment, she felt further away from solving this case than she had the very first day!

She was missing one vital link in the case— Stuart Feinstein. He had been with Annie on the night she was killed. *He* was Nancy's chief suspect. She decided that, after the memorial service, she would look for him once again.

"What do you expect to find here?" George asked as Nancy parked the rental car in the dirt drive beside Annie's cottage on Bodkin Point.

"I'm not sure," Nancy admitted, "but it's useless to go to Stuart's apartment. The police are staking it out, and besides, we've already searched the place. Maybe we can find something here that the police missed, a clue that will lead us to Stuart."

The front door was locked, but Nancy was able

to spring the bolt with the help of her lock-picking kit. Inside the cottage, Nancy took one look at the tidy living room, then frowned. "It's neat as a pin," she muttered. "You can tell that the police have already been here."

"We might as well give it one more look," George said, disappearing into the bedroom.

Starting with the cushions of the couch and ending with the kitchen drawers, Nancy searched the living room and kitchen.

"Any luck?" George called from the bedroom.

"No." Nancy took a seat at the kitchen table and looked up at the wall phone. Annie must have used it to call the police just before she was killed. There were no notepads to trace, no address books to study, but there was a wall calendar, compliments of Lenny's Bait and Tackle.

Wiping her hands on her jeans, George came into the kitchen. "Nothing helpful in the bedroom."

"I'm afraid the police have collected any evidence that might have helped us here. But we should make one more stop before we leave." Nancy nodded toward the calendar.

Confused, George stared at the wall, then grumbled, "Oh, no! Not that creep. I'm not crazy about guys who whip out their shotguns first and ask questions later."

"Come on," Nancy said, heading toward the door. "He might know something."

The girls walked up the dirt road to the wooden shack that housed Lenny's shop. Inside, they were greeted by Tyler, Lenny's gum-chewing son, who had let them "rent" the *Lazy Daze*.

"Not you again!" he said, glancing up from a comic book. "I'm still in trouble from the last time you came in here."

Ignoring his comment, Nancy asked about Lenny.

"He's in Florida for a fishing trip," Tyler answered. "But I'm not renting you a boat or equipment, either."

"We wanted to talk to Lenny about Annie Goldwyn," Nancy began. "She used to live—"

"I knew her," the boy interrupted. "But you're not getting a word out of me."

Nancy gave George a sidelong look. "Do you know something about the murder?" she asked Tyler pointedly.

"No, but I—no, forget it. I've got nothing to say." He sat down and held the comic book in front of his face. "If you want, you can come back next week when Lenny's here."

But Nancy couldn't wait that long. She had exactly one day to find Annie's killer before the press descended like vultures on Dr. Winston.

Outside, George turned to Nancy and muttered, "He's hiding something."

"I know." Stuffing her hands into her coat pockets, Nancy studied the bleak horizon. There were only three boats in the marina. Nancy's eyes widened as she glanced at the third boat. "Hey! That's the *Friendly Fin*. Annie's boat is here."

The girls walked over to the dock and studied

the cabin cruiser. "The police must have decided to store it here after they searched for evidence," George said, brushing her hair out of her eyes.

"It's sealed off." Nancy looked at the police tape that was wrapped around the doorway. It seemed to be loose, but she assumed that it had been torn away by the sea winds.

"Wait," George whispered, grabbing Nancy's arm. "I just saw the curtain move in that cabin window."

Nancy crept along the dock and stared into the cloudy window. Her eyes followed the pattern of a floral print curtain. At the edge of the curtain was a blue eye, peering back at her.

Nancy's heart raced. "There's somebody on Annie's boat." She stepped aboard, went down a few steps, and rapped on the cabin door, which was in the bow of the cruiser. "Open up!" she shouted.

The door didn't open while Nancy was banging on the door. George, standing on the dock, saw the hatch in the bow slowly open.

"Somebody's climbing out!" George shouted, racing down the dock.

Nancy jumped up on the dock again. She spotted a thin, lanky man climbing out the hatch. His back was to her, but as he straightened up, he turned, and Nancy got a look at his face. His hair was no longer blond, but there was no mistaking those bold blue eyes and high cheekbones.

Nancy gasped. "Stuart Feinstein!"

Chapter

Twelve

STUART TOOK a quick look at Nancy, then backed toward the dock on the other side of the cabin cruiser. "Leave me alone!" he growled.

"I just want to talk to you," Nancy said. "My name is Nancy Drew, and I was hired to help Annie."

Instantly, Stuart's mood softened. "I remember Annie mentioning your name. She told me that Winston had hired someone to straighten out this mess." He stared at Nancy and George for a long moment, as if deciding something. Then he motioned toward the cabin. "We should go inside out of the cold."

Nancy and George followed him down the steps that led below deck. They entered a small room in the center of which were a round wooden table and chairs. There was a built-in bench along one wall. Beyond that, Nancy could see a sleeping area.

"Now I know why that kid in the bait shop was acting so weird," said George.

"Who, Tyler?" Stuart shook his head. "That kid can't keep a secret to save his life. He knows I'm here, and he's just itching to tell everybody within ten miles. Fortunately, this place is pretty quiet in the winter."

"Well," said Nancy, "he didn't tell us much, but we could see that he was hiding something."

"I was jittery when I saw you two poking around outside," Stuart said, gesturing for the girls to be seated on the bench. "I've been hiding from some guy who's been trying to kill me, so—"

"Someone is trying to kill you?" George asked as she sat down on the upholstered bench.

Stuart nodded. "I think it's one of the guys who was hoisting barrels into the bay the night Annie was killed, but I can't be sure. Anyway, after the police questioned me on Tuesday, I went back to my apartment to sleep. That's when this guy jumped me right outside my place. I managed to give him the slip, and I've been in hiding ever since."

"Did you get a good look at him?" asked Nancy.

"Sure. He was a big guy, with short red hair, kind of a crew cut. I only got a look at him after I pulled off the ski mask he was wearing."

The ski mask! That's why Nancy had found it in the bushes outside Stuart's apartment. She was glad to have something to confirm his story.

Stuart sat down in one of the chairs by the table and rubbed his jaw. "I'd know him if I saw him again. He gave me a few good whacks before I got away."

Nancy nodded sympathetically. "Did you report him to the police?"

"What can they do?" Stuart asked cynically. "They couldn't help Annie when she needed it. I know the cops want to ask me some more questions." He frowned. "For all I know, they might charge me with Annie's murder. I don't have much confidence in the cops anymore. They can't stop Paperworks from ruining the bay, and they can't protect me from this guy who's out to get me."

"I know you work for the Mills Company," said Nancy, "but why do you think Paperworks is—"

"*Worked* for the Mills Company," Stuart said, interrupting her. "Right now I'm dead meat at that company. The bosses at Mills don't approve of the fact that I helped Annie with her stakeout. I wasn't a member of the task force, but I was willing to give up my job if Mills was tossing tires into the bay."

"That night on the bay—the night Annie died," Nancy said, "did you see who was dumping the barrels?"

"No," Stuart replied. "But I saw that they were dumping steel barrels, not tires. And I've also done some investigating since the night Annie was killed."

He picked up a leather wallet from the table and pulled out a plastic card. "This is my ID card from Mills. I changed the name and job title, and I dyed my hair."

"I thought you looked different," George said.

Nancy studied the ID card. "Simon Green," she read aloud, "Midwest Sales Representative." The photo on the card showed Stuart with the light brown hair that now fell over his eyes. "Do you mean to tell me that you're still working at Mills, under an assumed name?"

"No. I just forged this from my old ID card so that I could play detective for a few days," he said, waving off her question. "This ID card got me into a different branch of the company, the recycling center. I wanted to see for myself if things were legit. So I've spent the last two days spying on Mills. I pretended that I was Simon Green, visiting from Dayton, Ohio."

"Wow!" George said as she and Nancy exchanged an impressed look. "That's pretty cool."

Stuart shrugged. "I had to do something. I figured that if I could get some dirt on Mills, Annie wouldn't have died in vain."

"Is Mills guilty?" asked Nancy.

"Not at all," Stuart said. "In the two days that I spied on them, everything was on the level. They shred the tires down to crumbs right there in the factory. The crumbs are sold to road construction companies, who add it to asphalt."

Nancy nodded. "I've heard about that process. I also heard that it can be expensive."

"In time, they'll start to make money on it," Stuart explained. "While I was there, I even sneaked into their files to confirm the records. The recycling operation is working for Mills, Nancy."

"That means Mills isn't responsible for Annie's death," George said.

"And it points the finger at Paperworks." Nancy told Stuart about Paperworks's offer to buy the parcel of land at Terns Landing.

"That's it!" Furious, he paced to the window and pointed at the bay. "They'll take over that land and turn it into a waterfront dumping site."

"Not if the task force can stop them," Nancy reminded him.

Stuart was silent for a moment. "There's something you should know about the task force," he said quietly. "The police didn't think this was important, but it is. There's a rat on the force."

Taking a deep breath, Nancy nodded. "Yes, and it's someone who works at the aquarium. I've figured that much out, but I haven't worked out who it is. How did you know about the inside person?"

"That night, after we saw the guys tossing barrels in the bay, we went back to Annie's house to phone the police. I made the call, then went out to the main road to flag them down. Annie said she was going to call the task force and alert them. I don't know who she called, but I saw her dialing."

His eyes were sad as he added, "I didn't know she was going to play daredevil and take the *Fin* back out to watch the dumpers. Anyway, whoever she called must've radioed the guys on the boat. They killed Annie, then got away before the police arrived."

"You've suffered through a lot this week, Stuart," Nancy said sympathetically. "I wish you would give yourself a break and go to the police."

"No way." His blue eyes flashed with determination. "Not until the guy who tried to kill me has been caught."

As Nancy and George drove back into Baltimore City, they went over the details of the case.

"Who would Annie call?" Nancy asked. "Was there an established phone chain for the task force? Would she call the second in command?"

"Who also happened to be her closest colleague and best friend," George added.

Nancy stopped at a light, and the two girls looked at each other.

"Russ Farmer?"

By the time Nancy and George got back to the aquarium, it was late Thursday afternoon. The girls had gone straight to the mammal amphitheater to talk with Russ. They were sitting in his office, and Russ was wearing a wet suit for the presentation scheduled to begin within minutes.

"Yeah, I got the call, or at least my answering machine did," Russ explained. "But I wasn't home. I was here, working on a new routine with Schooner, one of the dolphins." His eyes were shadowed with regret. "I wish Annie had called me here. I'd have gone out there and kicked some—"

"Is there anyone else on the task force whom Annie would have called?" Nancy asked him.

"I don't know. Annie could have called anyone else in the group." Russ looked up at the clock, then added, "I've got to get going. You two staying for the show?"

"Sure," Nancy said.

"Are you going to be in it?" asked George.

"Oh, yeah," Russ said with a wide grin. "I'll be the one *without* the fins."

When the girls left Russ's office, they found that the amphitheater was nearly filled with excited, chattering people. They circled the huge pool, then climbed into the bleachers to find seats.

"Russ seems sincere," George said, taking a seat beside two girls wearing Whale Watch T-shirts.

Nancy agreed. "He's a sweetheart. I wish there was a way to prove that Russ wasn't home the night that Annie was killed."

A sudden hush fell over the crowd as a drum roll sounded. Suddenly the pool erupted, and a gray whale leapt out of the water, arching through the air before it splashed back down into the water.

"Welcome to Voices from the Sea," Doug said, speaking into a portable microphone. Doug and Megan climbed onto the platform that circled the pool. A second whale leapt out of the water, and the crowd applauded. "You've just met two of our beluga whales. Their names are Kia and Anore, and today they're going to show you that the underwater world is not the quiet place you imagine."

Dressed in wet suits, Doug and Megan went to the platform that jutted into the center of the pool, and the two whales joined them there.

"Beluga whales are often called sea canaries," explained Doug, "because of their constant chirping and squealing underwater." On cue, the two whales "spoke," letting out high-pitched noises.

"Anore is our largest whale, weighing in at eleven hundred pounds. She's going to demonstrate the power of the beluga whale's tail fin." Doug signaled Anore, and the whale rose out of the water as if she were standing on her tail. Moving her tail back and forth, Anore managed to walk backward in the water. "How's that for a moon walk?" asked Doug.

The audience roared with approval. Next Kia swam around the glass wall of the tank, pushing gallons of water out of the pool with her huge tail fin. Everyone laughed and squealed as the water splashed into the first few rows of the audience.

Looking down at the crowd, Nancy noticed a familiar face in the second row. "There's Detective DePaulo," she whispered to George.

"And he doesn't look too happy to have salt-water on his suit," George commented.

Considering the way this case was heating up, Nancy wasn't surprised to see the detective at the aquarium. Realizing that she had to tell him about finding Stuart, Nancy stood up and started down the aisle. "I'll be right back," she told George.

As the whales displayed their ability to find objects by sound waves, Nancy told Detective DePaulo that Stuart was hiding out on the *Friendly Fin.* "Stuart Feinstein is the prime suspect in a murder case," he said sternly. "He might have tried to hurt both you and your friend George!"

He calmed down when Nancy explained why she believed Stuart was innocent. By the end of the conversation, Nancy had convinced him to post a guard by the *Friendly Fin* and to hold off on arresting Stuart, just until Friday night.

As Nancy returned to her seat beside George, the whales leapt through the air for a final round of applause. Then Megan moved them to the adjoining tank, and Russ appeared, ushering in two dolphins.

"Meet Schooner and Nalu, two of our bottle-nose dolphins," said Doug. As Nancy watched, the dolphins leapt through the air. They were nearly as long as the whales, but their bodies were more streamlined, and their mouths and noses came to a point.

"For this part of the presentation," Doug explained, "our marine mammalogist, Russ

Farmer, is going to join the dolphins underwater."

At that, Russ took a running start and dove into the huge pool. Through the glass side of the tank, the crowd could see what was going on underwater. With strong strokes, Russ swam down toward the deep floor of the pool.

"Look," said George, "the dolphins are following Russ."

The audience gasped as the dolphins pressed their noses behind Russ's feet. They began pushing him through the water. They continued to push him along the glass wall, then nudged him up onto a platform before he ran out of breath.

"Now, if you watch closely," Doug teased, "you'll see the dolphins give Russ a little lift."

Once again, Russ dove down to the bottom of the pool. The dolphins joined him, placing their noses against the bottom of his feet. This time, they picked up speed until Russ arched toward the surface. A moment later, he was flying out of the water, propelled by the dolphins at his feet.

Awed by the spectacle of the grand finale, the crowd burst into applause.

"What a terrific show!" George exclaimed as she and Nancy filed out of the amphitheater. They headed back to the hotel to change for dinner. They had agreed to meet Chris and Jackson at a restaurant in the waterfront village of Fells Point.

As the girls passed the hotel desk, the clerk called out, "Miss Drew! There's a package here for you. It just arrived this afternoon." The clerk pointed to a long white box tied with a red satin ribbon.

"Roses?" George suggested, giving her friend a teasing grin.

It looked like roses. Smiling, Nancy was sure they were from the best boyfriend in the world, Ned Nickerson.

But as soon as she pulled the box across the counter, Nancy's nose wrinkled up in distaste. She had never received flowers that smelled so bad.

Nancy flipped open the lid of the box and gagged. Instead of fragrant roses, the tissue-lined carton was filled with dead fish!

Chapter

Thirteen

THAT'S DISGUSTING," George said, wrinkling her nose. "Who would do that?"

"There's a card." Nancy reached behind one silvery fishhead to remove the tiny white envelope. The message said: Back off or you'll be swimming with the fish.

Nancy glanced up at the clerk. "Do you remember who delivered these?"

"Sure," the young man said. "I signed for the box. It was brought by a messenger from one of the services used by lots of Baltimore businesses."

"That doesn't help us." Nancy tossed the card back into the carton, and the clerk promised to dispose of the offensive package.

"Someone really wants you off this case,"

George said as they rode the elevator up to their floor.

"I'll say. But I'm not backing off until I find out who killed Annie." Nancy's eyes flashed with determination. "This whole case is beginning to smell fishy!"

"Watch your step," Jackson said as Nancy and George negotiated a cobblestone lane of Fells Point. After a hearty meal at an old-fashioned colonial inn, the group had decided to take a walk along the waterfront.

Despite the wind off the harbor, the night was mild, and the seaport area was alive with the laughter and conversation of people on their way to restaurants and dance clubs.

Nancy was charmed by Fells Point, which resembled a seaport town from the turn of the century. Under the glow of quaint gas lamps, the group passed blocks of restored two-story brick buildings until they reached the docks, where two tugboats were moored.

Twinkling lights on the far side of the harbor caught Nancy's attention. "The bay is beautiful at night," she said.

"Very romantic, isn't it?" Chris agreed. "Unfortunately, the reality is harsh. Those yellow lights come from a sugar refinery. The green and white lights are a brewery, and the bright white lights mark the Paperworks plant."

"Wow," George muttered. "It's not so charming when you put it that way."

As the foursome looked out at the water,

various groups of people passed by. Turning away from the wind, Nancy glanced down the walkway just in time to see Megan walk by with an older woman.

"Hey! There's a familiar face," Chris said cheerfully.

"Hi!" Megan waved but kept on walking.

"Wait up!" Chris called jovially. "Aren't you going to introduce us to your lovely friend?"

At last the ladies paused. The older woman laughed and reached up to smooth back her red hair. "I'm not a friend, I'm her mother."

Nancy realized that the woman did look like an older version of Megan.

"It's nice to meet you, Mrs. O'Connor," said Jackson. "We work at the aquarium with Megan."

"Oh, my name isn't O'Connor. That was Megan's married name," the woman explained. "I'm Peggy Cribbins."

As Chris introduced Megan's mother to everyone in the group, Nancy gazed curiously at the older woman. She was sure that she had never met Megan's mother before, but both Megan and her mother reminded Nancy of someone else. She was still lost in thought when the women moved on and disappeared down the street.

"Megan looks a lot like her mother," George commented.

Jackson added, "She has a brother with the same coloring—those freckles and red hair."

"A brother?" Nancy said aloud. Her pulse began to race as the connection became clearer.

Cribbins . . . Daniel Cribbins! That was the name of the man she had run into at Paperworks. "That's right! Megan told me she had a brother!"

Confusion on their faces, the others stared at her.

"Nan," George asked, "what's going on?"

"Is her brother a big, stout guy named Daniel Cribbins?" Nancy asked Jackson.

He nodded. "Yeah, that's him."

"And he's employed by Paperworks?" she pressed.

Dumbfounded, Jackson and Chris exchanged a look. "I don't know about that," Chris said dubiously.

"Of course!" Nancy clapped her hands together excitedly. "I ran into him at the Paperworks factory. But I also saw him at the aquarium—in Megan's office. No wonder she didn't introduce him. Megan is Paperworks's inside link at the aquarium. She's got to be!"

"Do you think she's the one who put the ring on my air tank?" asked Chris.

Nancy nodded. "I'll bet she's the culprit behind most of the incidents at the aquarium."

"Although she couldn't have pushed you into the pool," George pointed out. "You said she was out in the office area with Russ."

"That's true," Nancy said, pausing to think back on that afternoon. "But that was the day I saw Daniel in her office. *He* could have pushed me into the pool, then dashed out of the area before anyone saw him."

Jackson still seemed shocked. "Do you really

think that Megan had the heart to kill those animals—the birds, and the porcupine fish?"

"I'm afraid so." Nancy frowned. "But she couldn't bear to kill one of the seals, whom she works with and is probably attached to. So instead, she stole Asia. It makes sense."

"My dad will want to hear about this," said Jackson.

"We'll give him a full update, first thing tomorrow morning," said Nancy.

"Then the case is solved?" asked Chris.

"Not yet," Nancy replied. "I need to collect the hard evidence." She looked at George. "That means we'll be paying Paperworks another visit. Tomorrow, right after our meeting with Dr. Winston, George and I will drive over to that plant across the water." She gestured at the white lights flickering across the bay. "But this time we're going in through the back door."

The next morning, when Nancy and George breezed into the private entrance of the aquarium, the security guard at the desk stopped them. "Excuse me, ladies, but I need to see your badges."

Nancy turned to show him her badge, and he waved her on. "Sorry, Miss Drew. You were in such a hurry, I didn't recognize you."

"Do you want us to sign in?" asked Nancy.

He waved her away. "No, the log book is only for after hours."

The girls were on their way up the stairs to Dr. Winston's office when a thought hit Nancy. "The log book! How could I have forgotten to check it! I can't believe it—I was so upset that I didn't remember to sign out, and the guard was so worried about my being caught in the net that he must have forgotten to remind me. I don't believe this—it was so obvious!"

"What? What are you talking about?" Confused, George followed as Nancy raced back down the stairs to the guard.

"I signed into the book the other night, when I came into the aquarium after hours," Nancy told him. "What about employees? Do they have to sign in and out?"

The guard nodded. "After hours, this is the only entrance that stays open, and everyone has to log in and out. The lobby doors, the emergency exits, the loading docks—they're all locked up."

"This was right before my eyes, and I missed it!" Nancy leaned against the counter. "Do you mind if I take a look at the log book?"

"No problem." The guard placed the book on the counter.

Nancy bit her lip as she leafed through the book, turning to the entries for Wednesday night. "Look, George. Chris isn't the only one who signed in the night that I was in the rain forest. Megan was here from seven until ten. She could have been the one who set the trap in the rain forest!"

Then Nancy turned back to Monday night— the night Annie was murdered. "Russ was working here the night Annie was killed, just as he said," Nancy confirmed, pointing to his signature in the book.

George looked at the entries over Nancy's shoulder. "But there's no entry for Megan that night."

"So Megan could have been the task force member Annie called after she and Stuart spotted the polluters." Nancy passed the book back to the security guard. "Hold on to this," she told him. "It's hard evidence."

"No problem," he said.

Upstairs, Jonathan Winston was encouraged by the progress the girls had made on the case. As he went off to meet with the party's caterer, he thanked Nancy for her hard work.

"We've got the puzzle solved," Nancy explained. "We just need to collect a few more of the pieces."

"At times like this, detective work should be called paper work," George said, closing the bottom file drawer and opening the drawer above it.

"Shh!" Nancy flipped through a hefty computer printout, then shoved it back into a file. "It's only four-thirty. The building is probably still filled with employees."

Working in the dim light of Paperworks's file room, the girls were methodically sifting through the company's records.

It hadn't been hard to sneak into the building. Nancy had pulled their rental car around to the rear of the factory, and she and George had slipped in through the loading dock when the workers weren't looking. The girls had even managed to elude the other plant workers. The problem was finding the documents they needed. They had been searching all day without success.

"I think we've been through almost every file in this place," George complained, standing up and stretching her back.

"I know," Nancy said, "but there's got to be something that proves Megan O'Connor is involved with Paperworks." She pulled out another printout and skimmed through it. "Something like—like a computer sheet with Megan's name printed across the top!" she gasped.

George rushed over to Nancy's side and read over her shoulder: "O'Connor, Megan—Miscellaneous Fees."

Nancy held up the printout, and three sheets unfolded with numerous columns of recorded payments. "According to this, Megan's been getting thousands of dollars from Paperworks. This is exactly what we needed to prove—"

Hearing a strange sound from behind a nearby door, Nancy paused.

"What was that?" George whispered.

This time they heard a scuffling noise from behind the door. "Look out!" Nancy gasped, pushing George out of the aisle. "Someone's coming!"

Chapter

Fourteen

HER HEART POUNDING, Nancy ducked behind a tall file cabinet in the center of the file room with George right behind her. Breathlessly, they waited for the intruder to enter.

A moment passed, and then they heard a barking sound, along with a dull thump on the door.

When nothing happened, Nancy's curiosity grew. She stood and edged toward the door. Cautiously she turned the knob. The door opened into a small dark room filled with boxes and a rack of blue uniforms. "It's a storage closet," she told George. Then, looking down, she saw two button eyes staring up at her. With a grunt, a seal pup wiggled out past Nancy's feet.

"Asia!" Nancy squatted down and stroked the seal between the eyes. "She seems to be okay.

Now we can tie the mishaps at the aquarium directly to Paperworks." She patted Asia's head. "When I think of how Megan shed those tears over Asia's disappearance, it really burns me up. She and her brother must have planned the whole thing!"

"She had all of us fooled," George admitted. "How are we going to sneak Asia out of here? We can't exactly hide an eighty-pound seal pup under our coats."

"Good point." Nancy peered into the dark closet where Asia had been held captive. On the floor she found two tins of water and a few scraps of raw fish. Along the wall, she spotted a row of blue coveralls on wire hangers. "Put this on," she said to George as she took a pair of coveralls off the rack.

Ten minutes later, Nancy and George were rolling Asia through the corridors, retracing their steps back toward Paperworks's loading docks. The girls had slipped on the coveralls, hoping to pass as plant employees. Asia was riding in a mail cart Nancy had commandeered from an empty office. Lured by a piece of raw fish, the seal pup had willingly climbed into a canvas mail sack.

To Nancy's relief, no one bothered them as they wheeled their precious cargo through the building. After riding the freight elevator to the ground floor, they maneuvered around giant parcels in the cavernous loading bay, and finally made it out one of the huge garage doors.

"Hey, where do you two think you're going?" A burly man in jeans and a black vest stopped them just outside the door. He was holding a clipboard.

"We have a special delivery to make," Nancy lied, thinking fast. "It's for Daniel Cribbins."

"Cribbins?" The foreman narrowed his eyes, looking from the mail bag to a list on his clipboard. "Okay. I know the guy."

Pushing the cart up to their car, Nancy and George loaded the seal and took off before the foreman had second thoughts.

By the time they arrived at the aquarium, the sun was setting. Thinking about Stuart, who was under police guard until the end of the day, Nancy pulled up on the walkway and parked right beside the seal pool. Then she and George carefully toted the mailbag containing the seal out of the car.

The guard came running out from the private entrance. "What's going on here? I saw your car on the monitor and— What's with the mail bag?"

After Nancy explained the situation, he helped the girls ease Asia back into the seal pool. As the pup splashed into the water, a few seals gathered near her, chortling and grunting.

"That is one happy seal family," said George. "Let's go tell Dr. Winston."

"He's in the lobby at the party," said the guard.

The party! Nancy had forgotten all about it. "I hope I can catch Megan," Nancy told George, "before she stages a catastrophe in front of the guests."

"I'll call Detective DePaulo," said George. "We'll need the police."

Inside the aquarium, Nancy wove through clusters of guests in elegant evening clothes. Finally clear of the party area, Nancy entered the causeway between the two buildings and broke into a run. When she reached the amphitheater, it was quiet except for the occasional splash or chirp of the dolphins and whales.

Russ wasn't in his office, but the light was on in the opposite office, and Nancy was surprised to find Megan sitting at her desk, writing notes on the whales' charts.

"Aren't you going to the party?" Nancy asked.

Megan looked up and blinked.

"I was sure you'd use the opportunity to cause some trouble," Nancy continued. "You know, push someone into a pool, kill one of the animals."

"What are you talking about?" Megan retorted.

"I've just come from Paperworks, where I found some records with your name on them," Nancy continued. "You've been on their payroll."

An angry blush stole across Megan's face. "I'm not a vicious person, Nancy. I had no choice. After my husband and I split up, I was left with a lot of debts. I needed the money that Paperworks could pay. All I had to do was join the task force and undermine their work."

Alone in her office, Megan looked thin and pathetic. "So all this is about those three hundred acres of land at Terns Landing?" asked Nancy.

Megan nodded. "The company needs that land."

"Not to mention the fact that if Annie pressed her case, your brother was going off to jail for illegal dumping in the bay," Nancy pointed out.

Megan's blush deepened. "Annie didn't understand how much Daniel had at stake," she insisted. "My brother was going to lose his job, along with the hefty bonus he got each year for keeping his department under budget. Daniel saved Paperworks money by getting rid of those barrels in the cheapest way—by dumping them into the bay himself."

"Don't you care about the animals at all?" Nancy challenged.

"I needed that money," Megan snapped. "None of us get big salaries here. When Annie stole that promotion away, well, it pushed me over the edge."

"You killed her over a promotion?" Nancy said.

"No, I didn't murder Annie," Megan muttered. "It was hard enough for me to kill those animals, especially when it came to the seals." Megan shook her head. "I just couldn't."

"So you took Asia from the seal pool and hid her at Paperworks," Nancy finished for her. "Don't worry, she's back in the seal pool now."

Megan stared down at her desk. "After everything I've been through, Asia is the only thing I care about at this aquarium." Muttering half to herself, she added, "I have half a mind to just take my seal pup and hightail it out of this state."

Nancy was surprised at Megan's attachment to the seal, despite all the cruel things she had done to other animals. Deep down, Nancy believed that Megan had some serious problems that weren't going to be solved by money.

"My sister is soft-hearted about these things," said a deep voice from the doorway.

Nancy spun around and found herself face-to-face with the burly, red-haired man she had seen in Megan's office, and again in the corridor at Paperworks. It was Daniel Cribbins, Megan's brother. Nancy took a few steps back, but Daniel was blocking the only exit.

"She didn't have trouble with the small things," he added, "like setting up that net in the rain forest and sending you those dead fish. Fortunately, I'm not as squeamish as Megan is."

Before Nancy could react, Daniel lunged toward her and clamped his muscular arms around her. "Get some of that rope from beside the pool," he barked at Megan as Nancy struggled to free herself.

Nancy managed to get one of her arms loose, but Daniel was too strong for her. In a matter of minutes, Daniel and Megan had Nancy restrained. Her wrists and ankles were bound with rope, and Daniel had tied her feet to one of the weights used to train the dolphins.

"You're not going to get away with this," Nancy warned them. "The police are closing in on you. If you turn yourselves in, you might—"

"The police don't have a case against us," Daniel insisted.

"They have solid evidence now," Nancy called out in a last ditch effort to change Daniel's mind. "They have documents and—"

"You're bluffing," Daniel said as he dragged Nancy over to the large, glass-sided pool. "But don't feel too bad. You've just saved a dolphin's life. When you burst in, I was back in the animal care complex, preparing a lethal injection. The party is moving into the amphitheater for a nine o'clock show, and we were sure that a dead dolphin would liven up the festivities."

He smiled. "Instead, tonight's grand finale will be a dead detective at the bottom of the pool. That will burst the task force's bubble."

"Wait a minute," Nancy said.

"Save your breath, Nancy. You'll need it." Daniel gave Nancy a shove, and she splashed into the water.

Frantically, Nancy kicked and wiggled, struggling to keep her head above water despite the bonds on her hands and feet. She was bobbing on the surface when she saw Daniel nudge the weight into the pool.

A moment later, she felt a tug on her feet. Nancy took a deep gulp of air before the sinking weight pulled her down. She sank like a stone, moored to the bottom of the tank. In another few minutes, she would be dead!

Chapter

Fifteen

THE AIR in Nancy's lungs dribbled out in tiny bubbles.

Her hair floated around her face as she looked frantically around the tank for a way to escape. Two of the dolphins circled, eyeing her curiously.

She was losing more and more precious air. Suddenly the dolphins paired off and swam up behind Nancy. One of them nudged her foot. As she watched, the two dolphins pressed their noses against her feet and pushed her through the water, dragging the weight along the bottom of the pool.

Nancy felt a glimmer of hope. This was the trick she had seen them perform with Russ! Could the dolphins push her to the surface, even with the heavy weight bogging her down?

Feeling as if her lungs were about to burst,

Nancy straightened out her legs, just the way Russ had locked his, and pointed her head toward the surface. A jolt of adrenaline shot through her as the dolphins nudged her again.

At first the progress was slow. Then the dolphins seemed to pick up speed, until they were pushing her, despite the weight trailing beneath her. At last Nancy was coursing through the water, rising up along the side of the pool, until she splashed through the surface.

"Ahhh!" She gulped the air, then threw her bound hands over the edge of the pool. With the weight at her feet, she couldn't pull herself out of the pool, but at least she could hold on to the side and catch her breath.

"Nancy!" George exclaimed. After calling the police, she had gone to look for Nancy. When George found Megan's office empty, she had decided to try the amphitheater.

"Get me out of here! Quick!" Nancy said breathlessly. She explained what had happened as George untied her hands. Next, George, fully clothed, dove into the pool to untie the weight. Soon Nancy was free.

"Detective DePaulo is on his way with two patrol cars," George explained. "But it looks like Megan and Daniel have slipped away."

"That young lady is dripping wet!" A woman in a green sequined gown glared at Nancy, who was trying to pass by the lobby without causing a stir.

"She's our resident mermaid," Chris said. He

excused himself and strode over to Nancy. "What's going on?"

"It's a long story." Nancy grabbed his tuxedo sleeve and tugged him out of the view of the party guests so that she could tell him what had happened. "The police are coming, but we don't want them to disrupt the party and alarm the guests. The problem is, Megan and Daniel have disappeared."

"I found them," George called from down the hall. "I told the security guard about Megan, and he said she's over by the seal pool with a van. She gave him some excuse, but she's trying to steal Asia again."

"We'd better get over to the seal pool," Chris said. "Come on, I can get us there through the back halls." The three of them raced up and down staircases and through halls until at last they reached the private entrance.

The first to reach the guard's desk, Nancy was surprised to see that it was empty. As she burst out the door to the seal pool, she found the guard passed out on the pavement.

"I gave him a nice dose of an animal tranquillizer." Standing on the platform in the seal pool Megan waved a syringe in the air. A portable medical kit lay open at her feet. "And I'll give you one, too, if you come any closer."

Daniel leaned out of a van, which was parked close to the seal pool. He groaned when he saw Nancy. "Not you again! Come on Megan, let's go!"

Stopping short, Nancy motioned for George to

stay behind her. She hoped that neither Megan nor her brother had seen her friend come out of the building. Right then surprise was her only weapon.

"I'm not going without Asia," Megan insisted as she leaned down to coax the seal pup onto the platform.

"Megan . . ." Clearly annoyed with his sister, Daniel jumped out of the van and climbed over the stone wall of the seal pool.

Chris used that moment to leap out from the doorway. Thinking fast, he jumped over the wall, grabbed a syringe from the kit, and jabbed it into the back of Daniel's shoulder.

"Hey!" Daniel bellowed, trying to twist away.

Nancy didn't waste a second. A few quick steps brought her to where Megan was still leaning over the pool. Nancy used a karate kick to knock the syringe out of Megan's hand. Set off-balance by the blow, Megan tumbled off the platform into the water.

"All right!" George said, rushing over to help Chris restrain Daniel while the injection took effect. "Will he be okay?" she asked.

Chris nodded. "It's a mild sedative that we use on animals. He'll be groggy, but he'll live."

"I just wanted to take Asia and leave." Megan stood in the pool, weeping. "I was sick of hurting people. I wanted it to be over."

"It will be," Detective DePaulo said as he came up the walkway. *"Everything* is over now."

Two patrol officers were right behind him. They lifted Megan from the pool and escorted her to a patrol car. Then Daniel was handcuffed and led away.

"Well," Detective DePaulo said. "I'm certainly sorry we missed *this* show!"

The party was such a hit that no one seemed to notice when two police cars and an ambulance pulled away from the seal pool. Nancy was happy to see the security guard come to as he was lifted onto a stretcher.

Still damp and shivering, Nancy and George retreated to Dr. Winston's office, where Chris brought them blankets and mugs of hot chocolate. Detective DePaulo followed them up to go over the case.

The detective didn't seem surprised when Nancy recounted all the evidence she had found —and the confessions of Megan and Daniel. "Once we get a look at their records, I think we'll see quite a few of the top people at Paperworks paying for the company's mistakes," DePaulo told Nancy, "and that deal on Terns Landing. There's no way the city will let that happen now."

"That's a relief," said George. "Was Lydia Cleveland in on the scheme?"

"No, it doesn't seem so," said DePaulo.

Chris gave Nancy's arm a squeeze. "Annie would be proud of you two," he said with a smile.

Dr. Winston entered, followed by Jackson carrying a tray of hot appetizers from the party. "I heard the news," said Dr. Winston. His gray eyes shone with gratitude. "I don't know how to thank you two."

"My only regret is that this case has wreaked havoc on my wardrobe." Detective DePaulo looked down at his leather shoes, which had been stained when he stepped in a puddle near the seal pool. "This is the third pair of Italian shoes that've been ruined by salt water."

Nancy glanced out the window at the inner harbor. "I'll be sorry to leave Baltimore. And I'll miss all the friends I've made here at the aquarium, especially the ones who saved my life."

"Don't mention it," Chris said modestly.

"I meant the dolphins!" Nancy quipped, smiling.

"Our return flight isn't until Monday," George reminded her. "We've got a few days left to do some sightseeing."

"And you know, we have a program called Aquadopt," Dr. Winston explained. "For a donation, you can adopt one of the animals here at the aquarium."

"Then count me in for two dolphins," said Nancy.

"And I'd like to adopt Ike." George smiled. "I've kind of grown attached to the big guy."

Nancy's next case:

Nancy's friend George is set to run in a Chicago marathon alongside some of the country's best female athletes. But Nancy soon discovers that running in this marathon could be hazardous to your health. Top runner Annette Lang has received a series of death threats—and she may be racing for her life!

The winner stands to take home some big bucks in endorsements, and where there's big money there's bound to be plenty of greed, trickery, and intrigue. Annette may be the best runner in the field, but it's Nancy who has to work fast. If she fails to catch up to the truth, at least one marathoner could end up dead in her tracks . . . in *RUNNING SCARED*, Case #69 in the Nancy Drew Files™.